# DOCTOR AGNÈS

## THE AGNES DUET #2

## HANNAH BYRON

Editor: Elaina Davidson
Cover Design: Poppet/Julia
More info: www.hannahbyron.com
ISBN eBook:978-90-830892-8-7
ISBN Paperback: 978-90-830892-6-3

"Forget safety. Live where you fear to live."

*~ Rumi ~*

# AUTHOR'S NOTE

The Edwardian novella *Miss Agnès* was originally published in 2016 with the title *The Blood Red Nails of War* as part of an Anthology with other authors.

I wrote *Miss Agnès* and this sequel *Doctor Agnès* as finger exercises for my *Resistance Girl Series*. They are only loosely related to the first book in that series, *In Picardy's Fields*, so if you've read that book, you'll find *The Agnès Duet* differs substantially.

*Miss Agnès* paints the prewar years of the French-Swedish Agnès Baroness Gunarsson de Melancourt and her rough-and-tumble with the freethinking inhabitants of Château de Dragancourt in Picardy: Elle and Jacques.

*Doctor Agnès* is about the young doctor's return to Château de Dragancourt in 1917. The castle has been transformed into a frontline hospital, but the same inhabitants are in charge. Can they come to terms with their past fallout in the middle of war?

I hope you will enjoy these rewritten novellas.

# 1

## A DOCTOR IN WARTIME PARIS

*Paris, July 1917*

On an early Friday morning in the summer of 1917 Agnès sat in the windowsill on the second floor of her father's house at the Place de Châtelet, overlooking the right bank of the River Seine.

The maid had opened the windows to let in the fresh air and the hubbub from the street below filled the room. It had rained during the night, leaving a soft mist over the world below, but the sun was rapidly covering the terrain. Coats already draped over lower arms and the waiters with their long white aprons were wiping the last drops of rain from the chairs and tables of the outdoor cafés.

There was a pensive look in the blue eyes of the young woman with her elegant blonde coiffure who'd just received her *Diplôme de ETAT de docteur en medicine* from *l'Université de Sorbonne*.

The young doctor was clearly lost in thought, paying only fleeting attention to Paris waking up to another day of war; a war both visible and invisible, as the City of Light had been under siege for three long years now but had not yet been captured by the Germans.

Visible were the bomb craters, the incessant stream of wounded men and the lack of almost all vital goods, the nightly raids and the constant blaring sirens. Invisible but as tangible were the fear, the grief and the dogged determination with which the Parisians shouldered their burden as they went about their daily lives.

Lessening some of that fear and pain was Doctor Agnès's job. Though not equipped with great physical ruggedness, Agnès had -despite her nymphlike, almost ethereal appearance - the inner strength of two buffalos. Her days all looked the same: wake up, put on her uniform, and set out to save lives at the American hospital at the Lycée Pasteur in Neuilly.

Only during this heavenly interlude before breakfast did she allow her thoughts to roam freely and dream of another life where peace reigned, and beauty and love returned.

In the other open window sat her best friend, Katell Brest, also a brand-new doctor with the same diploma. Katell was a bright, springy character with a mass of copper curls, slanted green eyes and a boyish figure. She originally came from Île-de-Ré and had lived at the Place de Châtelet with her Aunt Netty since her parents died seventeen years earlier. Katell was a matter of fact, what-you-see-is-what-you-get person, a counterpart to her philosophical and sensitive friend.

"Penny for your thoughts." Katell broke the silence.

"Sorry, was I daydreaming again? I do like to indulge in that before Justine taps on the door to tell us breakfast is ready."

"I must say I have no idea what you find to think about anymore. It's not like anything fun is happening that's worth my thoughts," Katell observed rather grimly.

"Oh you're right. I just can't help myself, Kat. Thinking is living for me, I guess. But I agree, there's not much hope for happier thoughts right now."

Used to her friend's philosophical musings - after all Agnès was a deep thinker and regularly contributed articles to *La Revue de Philosophie* as their youngest member ever - Katell broke her own gaze from the scenery below.

"I wish I had one ounce of your thinking capacity; I'm just sitting here, itching to get back to work. You know, I'm not very good at sitting still. Would never qualify as a Buddhist in the Himalayas." She chuckled, stretching her limbs while balancing on the windowsill.

Inseparable friends, though opposite characters, circumstances had forced them to live together. In the months leading up to Germany's declaration of war on France on 3 August 1914, their lives had turned topsy-turvy. For the first time, that spring, Agnès had not accompanied her father, the Baron Maximilian Dupuis de Melancourt, and his new wife to Sweden. Her studies at the Sorbonne had been more important than joining the annual family trip north to visit her mother's grave on Öland.

The Baron had agreed to Katell moving in with his adoptive daughter, so they could be looked after by Madame Proulx, the housekeeper, and the rest of the staff. The idea of living with her best friend had soothed Agnès sadness over not being able to travel with her family. And Kat had been as enthusiastic to set up house together.

But the war had changed everything for everyone.

Papa had married Agnès's mother's Swedish girl-hood friend in 1910, a widow called Elise Aberg with two children of her own. The family now couldn't return to France due to the war lines across Europe, and the Baron and his new family bided their time on Öland in the Baltic Sea, while young Agnès was by herself in Paris under siege. All made the best of it, though contact was irregular and far between. Agnès knew her father, who loved her like his own flesh and blood, was fretting and constantly worried about her.

Another reason to work as hard as she could and pray the war would be over soon. With most of their male colleagues enlisting as front-line doctors and field surgeons, every hand was necessary.

"So what were you thinking about?" Katell implored.

"Nothing too interesting. Just trying to grasp how all these countries are at war with each other and how we're sitting here seeing Paris wake up from a wet night. I cannot really fathom what a world war means and what how it will shape the future of humanity. What the rest of this century will look like." Agnès's chin rested on her drawn-up knees.

"Gosh, that's deep," Katell said with admiration in

her voice, "All I hope is that this relative peace will last another day in Paris. We never know whether the Hindenburg Line will hold. The Germans may still be marching on the Champs Elysées in August."

"That's just what I was thinking," Agnès replied, jumping off the windowsill and standing before her friend with her hands clasped before her, her stethoscope sticking out of her white coat. "I think we need to be where the real action is. Imagine what we could learn about our profession closer to the frontlines?"

"Are you kidding me? I think it's dangerous where we are right now. Spending most of our nights in your father's wine cellar by the light on one candle. It's quite enough adventure for me, trying to zigzag through the bombs the Germans are dropping on our heads every day."

"I know you're surprised to hear this from me, generally Miss Cautious ..." Agnès faltered, clearly doubting whether to speak her mind.

"What are you hinting at, Agnès dear?" Katell probed. "Just spit it out. We need to get going soon."

The creases in Agnès's forehead and the pursed lips displayed her state of contemplation. Blue eyes flickered, making clear she brooded over something. Agnès tended to fall silent when about to disclose an important decision, so it was Katell's role to give her the free pass.

"Ever since we got our diplomas, you've been talking of having doubts about staying put in Paris, but when I ask you where you want to go, you say 'nowhere in particular'. What do you want? Go to your father's castle in Picardy and enlist as a trench war doctor? Is that it?" Katell's eyebrows went up to her hairline.

"It is, actually." Agnès looked down at her hands. "How well you know me, Kat. I would go today if I could. It's my dearest wish to show that we women can also work on the frontlines, and I don't mean just the nurses, but us, doctors, next to our male colleagues." Her voice caught in her enthusiasm. "This is the Twentieth Century, after all; it will be *our* century, of women standing up for themselves, and we who have been educated at universities are the ones that need to set an example for other women."

She raised her gaze to looked at her friend imploringly. Katell wasn't in favor of her women's lib cause, she knew that, but Agnès had decided she wouldn't go without her. That was why she hadn't brought it up earlier, but the war showed no sign of coming to an end and she wanted so much to be in the thick of it, prove she could do it.

"Do you think your father would consent to you using Château de Melancourt as a base for your war effort?" Katell looked doubtful, avoiding a direct answer to her plea.

"That's been my other problem. That I can't reach Papa on short notice to talk it through. I'd dearly like to turn the Château into a temporary hospital for the wounded." Another deep wrinkle creased her fair brows.

"What was the first problem? I suppose that was persuading me to hop on board?" Katell, also in her white uniform, had left her spot at the window and stood well-grounded on the carpet, a mere one- meter-sixty tall but with mighty spirit and courage.

"I would never force you, but I can't go alone." She sounded tentative. "I need you, Kat, though I'd never wish to endanger you in any way. That's why I kept it to myself, but it occupies my thoughts all the time."

The girls looked at each other, closer even than many sisters, and with a deep affection and respect for each other.

Katell gave a short nod. "I go where you go, Agnès, simple as that. Though I don't know if I'm in favor of this latest craze of yours."

Agnès studied her; she knew her friend's loyalty and that she currently asked the highest price of her. "I think we'll be safe at Melancourt. I've studied the map with all the fronts. The castle is a good seventy miles south of the firing lines."

"But that can change anytime, right?" Katell observed drily.

"Sure, but we'll see it coming and will return to Paris if the lines don't hold. I don't want us to get killed. I just want us to help where help is needed most."

"I understand," Kat replied, "and I agree. We've got enough common sense not to do risky things. But I still wonder if your father would agree to all this."

At that moment Justine stuck her head around the door and announced breakfast.

As they sat down to their surrogate coffee and thin slice of bread and marmalade, the best the staff could do for the two young doctors with all the rationing, Agnès returned to their earlier conversation.

"Let's drive up to Melancourt on the weekend and see with our own eyes what's going on." And, with a glint in her eye, she proposed, "We'll stuff as many bandages and morphine and equipment in the Renault AX as we possibly can and leave it there for if and when we return."

EARLY ON SATURDAY MORNING, the two recently graduated female doctors embarked on their journey from Paris to the outskirts of Roye in Picardy, where the Château De Melancourt lay hidden in the green forests.

The Château staff had been kept to a minimum in the years the Baron had been abroad and Agnès was busy with her university studies, so the caretaker, Monsieur Legrand, walked around nervously opening the blinds in front of the windows, ordering his wife to secure the necessities to make sure the young Baroness and her friend were received in the order ordained to them.

But war and shortages in Paris had made Agnès give up all form of protocol. "Please, Monsieur Legrand," she pleaded, "we're not here to make things more difficult for you than they already are. We brought our own supplies from Paris." And deciding to take the bull by the horns, she added, "We are here to explore possibilities of offering our help as doctors to the front up north. What are your thoughts on us setting up a war hospital at Melancourt with your help?"

The old caretaker looked at her as if he'd swallowed poison.

"A war hospital, here, at Melancourt?" he repeated in great bewilderment. "What will the Baron have to say about that?"

Monsieur Legrand, who had been in the service of the Dupuis family when Max's father Alexandre was still the Baron, was a stocky man with a broad and ruddy face and grizzly beard. He took off his invariably black beret and scratched the short hair underneath. He looked positively disconcerted.

Kat kept quiet but Agnès felt for the old man. He was clearly not used to taking orders from women and certainly not from those forty years his junior.

"I understand that the idea of a hospital full of wounded soldiers is not what you envisaged, sir," she said in a friendly but decisive manner. "I also understand that you have plenty to do with looking after my father's tenants and generally just surviving these awful times, but we are doctors now and we have our duties, too. I promise I will bring enough staff, so the work for you and Madame Legrand will be kept to a minimum."

He cleared his throat. "Miss Agnès ... um ... Doctor de Melancourt, if I may, the front is at least seventy miles to the north and we in this DEPARTEMent would rather keep it that way. I've heard a large war hospital has been set up in Château Dragoncourt near Amiens. You could take a look there and see if your ... um ... skills, could be of use to that hospital?" It was the first time in nine years that Dragoncourt castle was mentioned in front of Agnès, and the name still hit her unpleasantly. Bad memories, bad people. But that was a long time ago and she had been another person back then, a mere girl.

Of course, Kat knew all about her fallout with the Dragoncourts, so she cut in, "I don't think that's a good idea, Agnès. Those people weren't very sound, if I remember correctly."

Agnès smiled. "Gosh, this is the first time I'm hearing about them again after all these years. You know what, Monsieur Legrand, Miss Katell and I will have our lunch under the oak tree in the garden and discuss what you've just told us."

Agnès's mind worked fast. She knew Katell was considering their options, too.

"It's really up to you, Agnès dear," Katell began once they had installed themselves in Agnès's favorite spot at Melancourt, "but to be honest, now we've traveled all this way, I'm rather curious to see those horrible twins with my own eyes. If they're still there, that is."

"Probably not," Agnès replied laughing. "I don't think they had one bone in their bodies that would consider the well-being of other people."

"But you always said the boy wasn't that bad," Kat probed.

"Jacques?" Agnès's eyes seemed far away for a moment. "He did apologize, that's right."

"Did you father ever mention if the castle was sold to another family?"

Agnès shook her head, "No, and it's not likely. The Dragoncourts have owned it since the Seventeenth Century. It's more likely hospital staff run the show there and the family is abroad."

Kat scrutinized her friend's face. "Do you think we should make the drive to investigate the place? If so, we'd better hurry up, to get back here before curfew starts."

"Let's hit the road to the palace of former horrors," Agnès giggled. "I actually can't wait to see if the only girl I ever punched in the face is still there, or long married to a boring Duke, with a trail of kids behind her."

"What was her name again?"

"Elle."

"I thought you said she wanted to become a race car driver?"

"Right, she did."

"And what about Jacques? How would you feel about seeing him again?"

Again Agnès face took on that pensive look and her corn-blue eyes betrayed a shadow of doubt. "Though he came off brash and overbearing at first, he was actually quite sweet when he drove me back to Melancourt that night."

"So?"

It was one of her and Kat's all-time favorite topics, discussing possible amorous affairs, as they were both still single at twenty-four. Their long studies and the war had proved finding a suitable husband harder than they'd imagined at eighteen, when they started their medical training. All young and eligible men had gone to war, leaving Paris to be ruled by women and men too old to fight.

Agnès shrugged. "Jacques was very good-looking, I have to admit that, but he also seemed the type that would not marry until the age of forty and the Earldom threatened to become extinct because there was no legal heir. You get what I'm saying? The sow- your-wild-oats first type."

"How exciting!" Kat clapped her hands, "Well, if your Jacques's still a bachelor and you don't want him, I'll take my chances."

"Kat, you wouldn't and it's in no way *my* Jacques!" Agnès cried out in mock despair. "But it does feel good to talk about this dark chapter in my life on a lighter note. Okay, so let's head over there and take stock."

"Professionally!" They said it in unison, semi-serious.

WITH KAT at the steering wheel of the Renault AX, Agnès couldn't help feeling some of the heaviness of the situation that nine years earlier had disrupted the peace and quiet of the secluded life with her father.

Her mind kept traveling back in time, despite her earlier bravado that it was all done and dusted. So much had happened that weekend, which had propelled her into early adulthood. And, soon after, the big next disruption in her life had taken place with her father's marriage to Elise Aberg. Suddenly she had a mother figure for the first time in her life, and a little sister and brother. Confusing times, which had increased with the outbreak of war.

Nine years of change and tumult, all beginning with her visit to Château de Dragoncourt and the wild twins. Was she coming full circle?

## 2

# THE WAY BACK

As they physically covered the distance between the two summer castles in Picardy, many of Agnès's important life decisions flashed through her. Her decision to study the human body and not be afraid of it anymore; to rip herself away from the dreamlife of stories and live in reality; to make a difference as an aristocrat instead of wasting a life in luxury, to embrace the liberation of women.

And now the war dragging on was changing everything. Even her oath not to go near Dragancourt ever again.

"You're okay?" Katell took her eyes from the road for a brief moment to glance at her friend.

Agnès smiled back at her. Kat intervened in her dismal thoughts at just the right moment. Sitting up a little straighter, she gave a small nod.

"Sure. I feel some apprehension going back to the place, in case the twins are still there. But it's been nine years. Lot of water under the bridge since."

"Did you ever hear from them again? Or bump into them in Paris?"

"No. I guess my guardian angels protected me from that," Agnès chuckled, "though I think I caught a glimpse of Elle at the Duke d'Orleans ball a couple of years back. There was a dark-haired girl in a male suit who looked quite like her, but I didn't take steps to verify whether it was so. The whole Agnès-befriends-the Dragancourt-children came to a screeching halt when Papa wrote a letter to their father explaining I wanted to refrain from further acquaintance with them. Without going into detail why, of course. I never told Papa everything. You know, the things I told you, that a stark-naked Elle sneaked into my bed in the middle of the night, and then almost suffocated me. I also toned down the blows I gave her. Papa would've made me go back and apologize in front of them if he'd known I'd hit one of the Dragancourt children." Agnès looked sad for a moment. "First time I didn't tell my father the whole truth about what happened in my life. Well, that's part of growing up, isn't it? Really, Kat, you're the only one who knows how I lost my so-called innocence though nothing truly improper happened. Gosh, I was such a ninny those days."

"You still are," Kat smirked.

"No, I'm not! I don't even bat an eyelash at seeing a body in state of undress anymore, now do I?"

"That's true."

"Well, if I'm attacked by the cat woman when we arrive and I end up in another scuffle, you are there to come and rescue me. I missed you so much that summer."

"And you think I'd do that?" Kat joked. "I think I will just sit down and watch the show, thank you very much."

"You wouldn't!" Agnès gave her friend a nudge. "Are you going to push me off the road now as well, Doctor Agnès? And here I was, thinking you such a meek, peace-loving creature."

At that moment Katell had to brake forcefully for the first roadblock they encountered since leaving Melancourt. They were stopped along the road by two French soldiers looking grim while clutching heavy machine guns against their chests.

"*Présentez vos* SAFE *conduits! Show your passes! Vous* ALLEZ *où?* Where are you going?" the first one asked. He looked tired but his face lit up at the sight of two pretty young women. "*S'il vous* PLAÎT," he added in a friendlier way as his superior trooped over to see what was going on with the two women in medical uniform.

"We're heading for the Château de Dragancourt. We were told it's been turned into a war hospital." Katell gave the soldier a kind smile, which he absorbed as a ray of sunlight.

His superior, a middle-aged Frenchman, who had an even more haggard face than his younger comrade, broke in, "The château is not a place for ladies like you. We even get sick to our stomachs when we have to go near the place, so I'd suggest you ladies turn around and go back to Paris."

"Don't underestimate us doctors, Sergeant," Agnès rebuked. "I can tell you we've already seen our fair share of casualties in the capital, so we're bracing ourselves for the worst. Can we pass?"

"If there's no holding you back, it's your call, but don't say I didn't warn you. *Et merci* BEAUCOUP. You are our only light in this endless darkness, doctors!"

And with that Agnès and Katell passed the first roadblock and found themselves entering the real battle zones of the North-French trench war.

While she looked out of the car window at the destruction and desolation on either side of the road, Agnes's earlier thoughts about a squabble over nudity with Elle and Jacques seemed utterly trivial, even banal. Whoever now ran the castle, she was prepared for the work, not to enter into failed former friendships.

AFTER CLERMONT, the roadblocks became more frequent and Katell had to answer the same questions, time and time again; it slowed the trip considerably and Agnès anxiously inspected the watch her father had given her for her graduation, a golden Elgin pocket watch.

"I know," Kat sighed, seeing Agnès's look stealthily at her timepiece, "but we can't go any faster, Aggie."

"In the worst-case scenario, if we can't be back at Melancourt before nightfall, we'll have to stay over at Dragancourt."

"If they'll have us," Katell muttered. "I'd rather not sleep in the fields here."

"Of course, they will. It would be terribly impolite to send us packing again. I'm glad we brought everything with us, just in case."

As they slowly progressed towards the northwest,

the girls fell into a silence, both too afflicted by the gloomy, godforsaken landscape they were transgressing.

It was like passing through a wasteland, one abandoned hamlet after the other with not a human being in sight. Houses and farms had collapsed under heavy cannon fire, and caught fire afterwards, ending up in black heaps of rubble with shards of broken glass jutting out, while ripped lace curtains flapped desolately in the wind.

Kat had to steer around bomb craters that appeared out of nowhere in the middle of the road, sometimes half covered with the debris of broken furniture.

Outside the villages the fields were scattered with charred tree trunks sticking up, like black fingers pointing to an angry god. The smell was pungent and sharp, a mixture of dust, gunpowder and teargas. The power of death was present everywhere, although still invisible to the eye.

The roar of approaching airplanes made them wake from the sights of horror. Deft chauffeur that she was, Kat gave a sudden, sharp jerk on the wheel and parked the Renault AX half inside an abandoned barn still covered with half a roof. They peeked anxiously through the roof tiles to the sky, relieved to distinguish the tricolor circles on the silver-colored planes.

"Thank God, Nieuports," Agnès muttered, "our compatriots."

"Yep," Katell agreed, rubbing the sweat off her palms.

"Right time to change. I'll drive the last stretch. You've done enough, Kat."

Her friend was so tired from the intense drive that she didn't even protest. Agnès took up her place in her father's car and reversed out of the barn for the last ten miles to Dragancourt.

"I'm not going to look at that spooky moon land-scape for another moment," Kat said, closing her eyes. "It's simply too horrible. I'd rather remember the lush countryside Picardy once was, where we played hide and seek, rode on horseback while the summers were long and warm and happy. Just tell me when we get to the place as I don't want to miss the first glimpse of the castle."

"I will, you rest for a while. I've got this."

As she steered the big car along the meandering roads, Agnès saw the first graveyards appear, some fresh, some older, rows and rows of white crosses, here and there a tiny bouquet of flowers attached to the cross or lying on the upturned soil.

*So, this is the real thing*, she thought. She felt torn about her plan now. Going back seemed no option but bringing herself and Katell into this hazardous situation was maybe not thought through enough.

Next to the dreadful sights, the stench got worse as well. At times Agnès had to put a handkerchief over her mouth. It was hard to determine what it was - burnt rubber, tear gas, gun powder - but whatever it was it made her nauseous.

Life had become quite incomprehensible. Whole nations fixed on killing off their able young men in the most horrendous ways. Armies fighting a ridiculous war in fields where there was nothing to be gained, no gold, no ore, no industry. It was just rolling hills of farmland and the glistening River Somme shimmering through the foliage. And she and Kat had to patch up these men that had fallen ... for what? For *WHAT*?

Suddenly, the Renault dove back into the shade of a long, winding road lined with old plane trees with fresh green leaves above army-camouflaged trunks. Here nature seemed unperturbed by the devastation around it, lush and whole, switching from one extreme to the next.

WHEN AGNÈS TOOK the D920 in the direction of Villers Bretonneux, their final destination, the war came close again, this time all-pervading, the rat-tat-tat of the machine guns, the cannon booms, the high, piercing whistling of shells. Then came the acrid smell of burnt materials - it was not clear whether it was human flesh, metal, garbage, or a mixture - permeated the car even with windows closed.

Soon after, the disastrous results of the war on human life became visible. For miles they had not seen a living soul, but now wounded men appeared every-where in the fields, some with missing arms or legs, bandages around their heads, lying on stretchers, or simply deposited on a blanket in the grass with Red Cross nurses and doctors walking among them, kneeling next to them, doing what they could to save lives or give the dying the little comfort they had in the form of morphine and prayer. The moans and cries that rose from the fields were a pitiful litany to the skies above.

Kat opened her eyes, blinking at the scene that seemed straight from Armageddon. "No!" She clamped a hand over her mouth. "How did this happen, how on earth?"

Agnès watched in silence, her eyes wide, as she maneuvered the car through the crowds, already itching to get out and help but knowing they could do nothing here but go on to Dragoncourt.

"Almost there," she said, swallowing.

And indeed, they saw the tall castle rise up before them as they took the last bend of the Rue Victor Hugo at Cachy.

Katell gasped and for a moment looked her usual happy self again as she exclaimed an astonished, "*Nom de dieu!*".

The sight of the castle in all its magnificence somehow threw Agnès back to her former self at fifteen, when her father told her all about Dragoncourt's splendor and its long history while they were having their tea in the conservatory of their own medieval castle. At the time she'd been mesmerized by his enthusiastic tale of the exquisite Renaissance architecture, the spooky underground tunnel and the family fortune. But for some reason, when she had finally been eye to eye with the château, she'd only focused on its inhabitants. Now she truly saw Dragancourt for the first time and she gasped as well.

Their awe was short-lived, though.

The closer they came, the more the lack of repair and neglect overshadowed the luster, but under the wear and tear it was still a magnificent building, with its walls and turreted roofs intact. The trees in the sloping gardens were standing in their original straight lines but now were formless and saggy, in need of a good clipping. The ponds were either drained or filled with murky green water, while the white plaster statues and rose arches bore some witness to their former glory.

The winged castle, though here and there in lack of paint, seemed untouched by the war, with its richly decorated walls of cream-colored stucco and gray-blue slated roofs, a myriad of round turrets and dormer windows, all of which were also adorned. On top of the highest turret an immense Red Cross flag flapped in the wind.

As they entered the driveway with its gravel path lined with box hedges that had once been cone-shaped, the real change became apparent. It was not the building; it was what happened in it and around it. There were wounded men everywhere on the lawns, those who could not walk having been wheeled out in chairs or beds. Nurses with white headbands and red crosses on their white-aproned bosoms walked among the mutilated men like floating angels. Despite the sunshine and the smiling women, there was a dreariness to the scene that struck Agnès more than all the other images so far.

Nothing at Dragoncourt would be as it had been before the war.

Kat in the passenger seat looked dazed and kept muttering under her breath, "Goodness gracious, who would've thought."

"Quite different from Paris, isn't it? There we still had some semblance of order, but this is just complete chaos," Agnès observed, as she looked for a spot to park the car.

She had to zigzag through the crowds and vehicles at walking pace. All possible places seemed taken by military trucks and Model T Ford ambulances. Even one of Madame Curie's mobile X-Ray vans was parked on the gravel along the front side of the castle.

Two tired, frazzled young doctors disembarked from the car and stared at each other.

"I don't know if I've done the right thing, suggesting this," Agnès started hesitantly. "Maybe ..." Kat walked around the car and slipped her arm through her friend's. "Don't you dare retrace your steps, Agnès Gunarsson de Melancourt. We've come this far. Now we're going to fulfil our duty."

## 3

# CHÂTEAU DE DRAGANCOURT

J ust when Agnès and Katell wanted to head towards the castle's entrance, they had to jump back, unexpectedly overtaken by one of the black ambulances at high speed. Its braking tires threw the gravel into the air as it came to a screeching halt before them.

"Heavens," Katell exclaimed, "I didn't see that one coming."

The driver, a woman wearing a male khaki uniform with a red cross, sped out to open the back of the ambulance. Another woman in the same uniform crawled out. Grabbing the handles of a stretcher they ran up the steps with a heavily bleeding man in a gray-blue uniform and disappeared into the castle. It all happened in seconds, an almost surreal undertaking.

*They were women*! flashed through Agnès. *Strong women doing* A MAN'S TASK.

And then it dawned on her. Thinner, grimmer and without any finery.

"I think ... I think the dark-haired driver was Elle."

Katell fixed an intense green stare on the place where the woman had disappeared.

"Heavens," she observed again, "I didn't get a chance to see more than a glimpse of her, but that would mean ... you know?"

Agnès nodded. "Well, Elle always loved driving dangerously, so it looks like she's found her métier. I'd rather pictured her in a gleaming Mercedes Benz taking part in the races of Le Mans than trudging through Picardy in a delipidated ambulance. Guess the war's changed things for her as well."

"You still want to go ahead with this?" Katell scrutinized her friend's face.

"Sure. Let's go!" Agnès grabbed her medical bag that doubled as her handbag from the back seat and locked the car. "Dragancourt, here we come!"

WHAT THEY SAW when they entered the large central hall with the high ceiling full of stucco cherubs and grapevines was a sight Agnès was sure would be branded on her retinas for the rest of her life.

All human senses were stretched here to the extreme. It was absolute chaos. The wounded lay everywhere, on beds, blankets, tables, even on the marble floor, and their screaming tugged on the doctors' hearts. The predominant color was red, human blood, and it had stained the carpets, the clothes of both patients and medical staff, even the walls. The smell of decay and terrified sweat permeated their nostrils.

Nurses and volunteers were running around carrying the wounded from the central hall to what Agnès supposed were the wards and the operation rooms.

While they stood transfixed, at least three new wounded men were hurried in. Despite the frenzied activity of the stretcher bearers almost bumping into each other, avoiding each other at the last moment, somehow this operation worked in the chaos in which it took place.

Nobody seemed to take notice of two new female doctors standing timidly between the marble columns, their medical bags clutched in front of them. If they'd had it in their minds to strip the walls from their precious paintings and run away with them, nobody would probably have lifted one finger. It was a strange paradox of human pain and age-old art, a place where only one law was still operations: relieve the suffering.

"Let's go," Agnès finally said. "I think I know where they're taking them."

Stepping over moaning bodies as well as corpses, around pools of blood, avoiding as best as they could the overwrought nurses, Agnès led the way in the same direction as Count Horace had once taken her, to the castle's hub, it's magnificent dining room, where at least fifty guests could be seated around the extended dining table.

Agnès was bracing herself for what it had been turned into. "I guess we'll have to head towards LA *gr*ANDE SALLE *verte*. Seems like the only place large enough to set up a temporary operating theatre."

Katell, though not of noble birth herself, had been such an integrated part of the Dupuis de Melancourt household that she knew what the inside of France's aristocratic places looked like. As they flattened themselves against the wall to let more stretcher bearers flee past, she said, in an attempt to lighten the atmosphere a little, "Probably as big as one of the operation rooms at the American Hospital but with more luster."

"Indeed," she agreed, "and somehow it feels fitting to use these grand SALLES for war purposes today. Human abundance brought to its knees."

Agnès cautiously opened the ornate door that entered the green room. There was no one guarding the entrance, so they shuffled in as silently as elves, once again taking stock of the situation with a professional eye. She'd been right. Big lamps had replaced the crystal chandeliers and on one side of the immense oval table two doctors and two nurses stood with a concentrated frown between their brows, bent over that part of the operating table that was covered with a green rubber mat.

There was a sudden stillness in this high- ceilinged room when compared to the entrance hall and corridors. Here the two wounded men on the table were silent, sedated on high doses of morphine. Only now and then a muffled moan escaped.

Uncertain how to proceed, Agnès and Katell lingered near the entrance.

"So much work to be done here," Katell whispered. "We could easily work on the other side of the table. Enough wounded here that need our attention."

"Far too many for these two doctors, "Agnès agreed.

At that moment she saw a tall young man with an unruly mop of dark hair and a pair of silver-rimmed spectacles come their way. His white coat had some bloody spots but was not as smeared as the others.

*Another doctor?* she wondered but he somehow didn't fit the bill. There was a look of numbed terror in his brown eyes as if he had lost the capacity to really take in that what was going on around him.

"Can I help you, ladies? Have you been sent here by anyone?" Pointing to their bags, he understood they were doctors.

"Jacques?" Agnès gasped, as the pieces of the puzzle fell into place in her mind.

For a moment he looked at her with the same unseeing eyes with which he inspected everything around him, but then the light switched on in his eyes. "Agnès!" he exclaimed, a beaming smile breaking over his joyless face. "Agnès Gunársson. Bless my bark!" He pronounced her Swedish name, which nobody seemed to use these days, in a singsong way.

They stood staring at each other for what seemed an eternity and a strange tremor went through Agnès she could not control. It made her tongue-tied. Here was this tall and handsome man, exuding a devilish combination of restrained wildness and confused curiosity. His sudden appearance before her catapulted her back in time. Unwillingly, as that kind of awkward teenager was not what she wanted to be, certainly not in this situation.

Though the years had changed him, traces of his troublesome years remained in those dark eyes, though his general demeanor seemed more serious and focused. The glasses were new, as was the permanent line etched between his brows.

Having neither expected to seem him so soon and so changed, she answered almost shrilly. "Yes, it's me. Jacques, I've become a doctor. And this is my friend and colleague Katell Brest."

Jacques also snapped out of his shock at seeing her and, clamping the clipboard he'd been carrying under his armpit, shook their hands in a cordial manner.

"Does it mean ... does it mean, you two showing up here, that you would want to come and help us? But why didn't you give us a ring. We would have been better prepared. Sorry for my rambling, so surprised."

Agnès and Katell exchanged glances.

"There is a possibility we will stay," Agnès replied. "We've just come from Melancourt. My initial idea was to turn that into a temporary hospital. Then we heard there was an operational front- line hospital here at Dragancourt, so that's why we ..."

"Wonderful!" Jacques exclaimed. "If you give me a sec, I'll show you around." Then his face fell. "You know Elle's still here? She's very much part of the team as an ambulance driver."

Agnès nodded. "I think I saw her in that function already. It's no problem, Jacques. My childhood vow never to return here was taken in a different epoch. All that matters now is to employ our services where they're needed most."

Agnès felt Katell's gaze on her and she gave her a brave smile that signaled *it's OKAY*. She didn't miss the *OH-LA-LA* look and the way Kat batted her lashes. She was clearly taken by Jacques's attractiveness. Agnès hoped the man in question had missed the feminine hints.

Jacques, true to his maleness, continued unperturbed, "Great stuff! In any case, we absolutely need to find a quiet place in this madness to have a chat first before the tour, explain my part in it as well. If it isn't apparent." He laughed drily.

"Alright," Agnès and Katell agreed in chorus. "And I could really do with a cup of strong coffee before we roll up our sleeves," Katell put forward.

Her matter-of-fact voice had the immediate effect of grounding Agnès.

"So you think–" Agnès began, but Katell cut her short.

"We've got a few hours of daylight left before we return to Melancourt. Why not make the most of it?"

Agnès saw Jacques's eyes light up.

"In that case, coffee it is. As much as you like," he said with more gusto. "Let me show you our current quarters. It's very different from when you ... uh ... stayed here, Agnès, but we have to make do with what we've got left."

Leading them through the corridors away from LA grANDE SALLE verte, Jacques took them to the same garden room where Agnès had conversed with his father nine year earlier. A strange duality befell her.

For a moment she felt the spirit of her old dog Gåva, who had died shortly after the disastrous weekend she'd spent with the twins. It felt as if the spirit of her loyal dog had sent her here, to set matters right. As always, her heart bled when she thought of Gåva, but she pushed the thought aside. Mourning her dog who had died peacefully of old age seemed almost inappropriate among the suffering of men in

their prime, one after the other the light in their eyes
dying.

She was glad to enter the room bathing in the warm
July light. *La salle de jardin* was a sunny room by all
standards but this afternoon in particular a golden
aureole set the walls and the furniture ablaze. After the
grim, dark-red and gray ambience they had encountered so far inside the castle, it was a welcome change.

Agnes remembered it also as the only room in
Dragancourt she associated with pleasant memories.
Here she had sat talking and drinking tea with the
amiable but sad Count, the twin's father, given a
momentary release from Jacques and Elle's constant
provocations. In their father's presence they, too, had
showed a little more respect and a little less clamoring
with each other, turning into passive spectators. The
memory made her smile.

Jacques clearly felt some of her conflicting
emotions as he came over to her, taking both her hands
in his. The palms of his hand were warm and
comforting,

"Thank you for coming, Agnès, I'd never in a thou-
sand years would've dared to dream you'd be standing
in this room again."

She saw he was struggling with his emotions, the
Adam's apple moving in his throat, his round glasses
misting up. She gave his hands a little squeeze. "Neither
did I. Let's call it providence."

"I'm afraid we'll have little time to catch up on the
years, but I must disclose a secret. I knew you'd studied
medicine at the Sorbonne and became a doctor. I
couldn't help myself pulling at the strings of some of

our mutual acquaintances in the capital to get some news about you." He looked endearingly sweet as he confessed this.

Agnès withdrew her hands but kept smiling. "I'm afraid I can't confess a similar crime, Jacques. I told Kat I didn't even believe you'd still be here at Dragancourt."

"Have we fallen so short of your expectation?"

Seeing Jacques like this, nothing like the indolent teenager he'd been, but a man with a warm beating heart, helping others in distress and trusting this whole estate to the war, made her look up into his eyes again.

"I'm sorry," she said softly, "let bygones be bygones. It's of no consequence anymore."

"Gosh, you've changed so much," Jacques observed, walking away from her to the percolator on the side table, "I still pictured that waiflike, ethereal being who seemed more to float through the air than walk on the earth." He kept talking with his back to them as if disclosing this information to her face was too much for him. "And here you are, solid, practical and more grounded and confident than Elle and me together. I still can't believe it's you."

Glancing over his shoulder, Jacques said on a more light-hearted tone, "Well, never mind me. Do sit down, doctors. Let the Count serve the ladies coffee."

This disclosure brought another realization. So far, they'd not seen one servant where usually the place had been full of maids in black dresses and white aprons and footmen in livery. War had changed this. Before the servants would have outnumbered the family members by far, now all seemed gone. It had thrown their generation, who'd all been brought up without having to do any house- hold chores, into a new era.

While Jacques busied himself with the coffee, they sat down, side by side on the sofa in the bay window. Katell gave Agnès one of her tell-tale looks.

"Don't," she mouthed.

Kat refrained from commenting but smiled affably.

Agnès took the moment of quiet to glance around the sunlit room. It was clearly used as a recuperation space for the family and possibly the medical staff. It had a more practical arrangement than she remembered, with a long table along the back wall, which held two percolators for coffee, tea pots, cups and saucers and slices of chocolate cake and buns under bell glasses. The same Renoirs, Monets, and Van Goghs hung on the walls and Agnès recognized the bone china service set and the gray leather lounge chairs. The familiarity of this touched her and she could almost see the old Count sitting there, twisting his moustache, his sad eyes resting with disbelief on his unruly offspring. Somehow, they had been so close for such a short period of time, and it was only now that it occurred to her.

"Where are your father and mother, Jacques?"

The question had escaped her before she could check herself.

He threw her a glance over his shoulder and that was strangely familiar, the dark lock of hair over one eye, the conflict in the gaze always at bay.

"Father's in London, wants to retire as the French ambassador, but Clemenceau doesn't want to hear about it so he bides his time there. Mother's with him at times but is mostly at her own estate near Canterbury. They're safe at least."

He sighed, putting down the steaming cups on the coffee table in front of them. The tone in his voice made Agnès decide not to probe any further.

"What about your father, Agnès? I heard he got married. That must have been a change for you?"

"It was," she agreed, "but in a good way. I've known MAMAN Elise and her children since I was a little girl. I even vaguely remember her husband who passed away when I was four. We always visited her when we visited Mama's grave. MAMAN Elise was the only friend that stood by my mother, you know ... uh ... well, that's another story."

Agnès was aware that the same uncertain, childlike version of herself returned to the room and she swallowed. She didn't want to disclose more about her mother, or the complex situation in which the Baron had decided to marry the widowed Elise Aberg and become the father of a total of three adoptive Swedish children.

Jacques, sensing her discomfort, came to her rescue. "Oh, Agnès, I'm so sorry. I shouldn't have asked you about your family. Maybe one day you'll tell me what happened to your mother, but I agree, now isn't the moment. I'm also being rude to Katell, who's completely shut out of our conversation."

"Not at all!" Katell's clear voice broke in. "There's one thing you must understand, Monsieur Jacques. Agnès and I are like sisters, so no amount of time you two talk about the past can ever bore or disinterest me.

On the contrary." Her green eyes flashed at him in a playful manner.

"Please drop the Monsieur," Jacques replied, clearly relieved at Katell's interjection.

"It's still surreal to be back here, Jacques, certainly in these circumstances," Agnès observed after a silence. "I remember everything as it was, everything about you as well."

"Your words lift my spirit in more than one way, Agnès." he said gratefully. "With the hell that's been going on here for almost three years now, that's like balm on my soul. I never realized until today that there was a minor private war that Elle and I still hadn't settled and that was with and over you. Hope- fully, we can make it up to you this time."

Agnès nodded. "I'm looking forward to seeing Elle again. And I promise you I won't punch your sister in the face again."

"Oh, you have my consent," Jacques chuckled but then his face turned serious, "though I think you wouldn't recognize the old Elle. She's one of the rocks on which this operation rests." He looked ever so proud as he spoke of his twin sister.

# 4

## THE POWER OF WOMEN

They were seated as they had done nine years earlier, only now with Jacques sitting in his father's chair. The coffee was strong and bitter, just what Agnès needed.

After she'd eagerly drowned the first cup, she asked, "So if we come to an agreement, would you have need for two more doctors?"

"Need?" he cried out. "We're short-staffed every single day. Nurses still come and offer their services, but it's doctors we lack most. At the moment we only have two, whereas we generally have at least fifty wounded men per day. Doctor Renard and Doctor Morrisette are at the end of their ropes so your offer's absolutely heaven sent. We've been near the front lines for three terribly long years now and there are hardly any hospitals in Picardy itself.

Those that can be transported to Amiens or Paris are taken there, so here we get the really severe cases that can't be taken too far without risk. I take it you can do surgery?"

"It's not our main expertise," Katell disclosed. "We've been trained as general doctors, but under the circumstances we'll do what we can."

"We've learned so much from our work in the hospital in Paris, ever since we started there as trainees. We tend to learn things on the job these days. In the old days, we'd not be supposed to undertake surgical interventions we hadn't practiced under supervision, but now we have no choice. Luckily, we're both fast learners," Agnès explained further.

Jacques nodded and then checked his wristwatch. A worried look glided over his tired face as he fixed his gaze on Agnès. "I wish I had more time to show you both around, also explain what *my* job here is, but Elle will be arriving any minute now. I'm taking over her ambulance shift to the trenches. The poor thing's been working since daybreak. She and Abby ..."

At that moment the door swung open and, in the doorway, stood Elle in her khaki uniform, a leather belt around her slender waist and her wide trousers in firm leather boots, her cap between fingers that still had the painted red nails. She was followed by a wiry looking woman in the same uniform, at least a head shorter than Elle with a friendly round face and wavy shoulder-length, brown hair.

Agnès slowly rose from her chair and the two uniformed ladies, one the ambulance driver, the other a doctor, stood staring at each other. Agnès saw the topaz eyes take on a surprised look but the memory did not click immediately. Then in a flash it did.

"Do you remember me?" she asked, holding out her hand.

"Of course I do. I'd be sorry if I didn't." Elle shook the hand briefly, but quickly averted her gaze to the wiry young woman who had come up next to her. "This is Abby, Abigail McAllister, my anchor in the madness."

They all shook hands.

The first thing Agnès's professional eye noticed in her old foe was that she was overwrought and skittish from exhaustion. Elle's eyes, though still a deep topaz, had the same numb expression as Jacques's had at first and her eye sockets were a matted brown. She was also too thin inside that unflattering uniform.

From her course in psychiatry, Agnès knew that if the brain was exposed to too many horrific images over too long a period, it copped out and both thoughts and feelings became dulled and monotonous. In order to cope with reality, one shut down. This had happened to both the twins, whose youth had been all about bright colors and abundance with not a care in the world. They'd never been trained for such a hard life and adaptation was even more difficult for them.

Physically, Elle had also aged beyond her twenty-seven years, but she was still a beautiful aristocrat with that regal flair and glimpses of that overbearing confidence. A tough cookie indeed. Even the red band on her forehead where her cap had been and the stains on her tunic looked on Elle as if it was the latest Paris fashion.

Agnès became aware she was once again gaping at this magnificent girl, as if she were fifteen years old again. To break her own spell, she said, "Sorry that

Katell and I just arrived on your doorstep without announcing our arrival but we're here to offer our services."

The flashing topaz gaze went up and down, taking in Doctor de Melancourt. Agnès saw admiration and bewilderment in Elle's glance.

"Heavens, girl!" she exclaimed with some of her former exuberance. "A doctor? Who'd thought that? Not me! Oh, wait a minute, Jacques told me something of the kind years ago, didn't you, bro?" She slapped the forehead with the red band. "Geez, sorry, slipped my mind. Well, welcome to the club. Not that

J. and I are doctors, but Abigail here's a nurse." And turning to her anchor, Elle added, "Abby, this is an old ... uh ... friend and her colleague. Well, I need a coffee. Ab, you want some?"

Elle was already sauntering over to the percolator with that peculiar gait of hers, feminine and tomboyish at the same time.

While she and Abigail dropped onto the leather chairs, Agnès and Katell retreated to the sofa. Agnès felt Katell's burning eyes on her but didn't look her friend's way. She wasn't sure what grimace she would make this time.

Elle stretched her khaki legs, crossing them at the knee. Her boots were muddy and stained the carpet, but nobody seemed to care.

"You'll have to do two more drives to Albert before dark, Jacques, unless ..." she gazed in Agnès's direction, "... you want to stay here. I can do them." With a familiar movement, Elle retrieved a cigarette from her silver case, tapping the stub on the smooth surface.

Her brother hastened to offer her a light. "I'll do them, Elle. I was just telling Agnès and Katell I'd have to leave. You rest now, sister, and get some sleep before dinner."

"Alright. Thanks. Just watch out when you cross the River Somme. It's infested with German snipers." Her voice was flat, nothing of their former fights sounded through, only cooperation.

"You don't have to worry about me. I thought you knew that by now." And turning to Agnès and Katell, he invited, "Do stay for dinner. There's not much we can offer but we still have Dolly here with us and she still puts together a mean *Poulet Basquaise*. Though the chicken tastes more like rubber band these days. But she does the best she can."

Agnès and Katell looked at each other and nodded.

"We can stay for sure, if you let us do some work for our keep." Agnès said in an attempt to be light-hearted.

The twins stared in their direction.

"Do you mean you'd like to stay straightaway? We can certainly accommodate you for the night, but I thought ... I thought you'd probably have to go back to Paris?" Jacques ventured.

"We set out to Picardy with the intention of seeing if we could be of any help here. So why go back if there's so much to be done immediately? Although Paris isn't occupied, we're used to living under war conditions, so we don't expect much."

"We've spent half of our days in the Baron's wine cellar," Katell added, "both studying and sleeping there. That's Paris for you these days. Constant bomb alarms."

Through the smoke Elle was observing Agnès and
Katell with squinted eyes, clearly weighing the change
in atmosphere if two female doctors were to strengthen
their ranks.

In a slow, raspy voice, she commented, "I'm all for it.
God knows Renard and Morrissette can do with extra
pairs of hands. What about you, Jacques, Abby?"

"Where will they sleep? Our quarters are cramped
as they are."

It was the first time Abigail took part in the conversation. Agnès was surprised to hear she was American.

"We'll open two more rooms on the first floor, don't
worry," Jacques replied. "I'll ask Guillaume to see to it."

"One room is enough. Kat and I are used to sharing
a room." This earned her another hard stare from Elle,
but she ignored it. "So your butler is still here?"

Agnès remembered the stiff man in his black livery
with his invariably alert look as if someone would
shout 'catastrophe' behind him any minute.

"Sure," Jacques replied, "though Willy wouldn't be
pleased to be labeled 'butler' anymore. These days we
call him steward Guillaume. Can you ask Willy to
prepare a room, Elle? I've got to change and dash out."

"Sure," Elle extinguished her cigarette, "if you two
have made up your mind that you want to get really
dirty?" She turned to face them, dark eyebrows raised.

Agnès echoed her with a curt, "Sure."

Jacques raised from his chair. "I'll see you all at
dinner, ladies. No formalities needed anymore."

They all laughed, recalling dress codes before the
war. But silence fell over the room after the only male
had left. Some of the former awkwardness Agnès had

felt during her first visit to the château began to creep in.

Katell, always sensitive to her friend's state of mind, broke the tension. "I'm not worried what I'll get in my stomach later or where I'll put down my head, I'd really like us to get to work. We've been idling all day long and that's not our style."

Abigail sprang to her feet. "I'll show them around, Elle. You take a break." Elle open her mouth to protest but the American put her firm hand on Elle's thin shoulder. "You have a bath and a nap, honey. I've got this. Ladies, if you'd follow me?"

Elle consented grudgingly, her full lips curling at the edges. "Thanks, Abby, though I'll never understand where you get your energy from. You've done the exact same shift as me and you're still as fresh as the morning."

"American make-believe, darling. We're good at pretending we're larger-than-life." With those words she ushered the two doctors out of the door and back into the direction of the hospital quarters.

AGNÈS AND KATELL had not had the opportunity to discuss this sudden new direction their lives were taking but they let themselves be led by the fiery American nurse.

Katell asked Abigail, "So how did you end up here, Nurse Abigail?"

"Just Abigail or Abby, please. Rule 1." She raised a tapered finger. "In our little circle we don't use titles,

professional or otherwise. Or we'd be saying count and
countess all day, and doctor such and nurse such. Only
when we're around patients we act as if we're polite
folk. But to answer your question. Elle and I met in
New York before the war. We became best pals, so it
was only logical that with my nursing skills I offered to
come and help out here. Arrived here in the Fall of 1914.
Saw the first batch of fallen men, right from the start."
She nodded her wavy hair, a sad look in the oval gray
eyes.

The way she said 'best pals' sounded very intimate.
It made Agnès wonder what sort of relationship she
and Elle had. *None of your business*, the little voice in her
head whispered.

Pushing the Dragancourts and their affairs to the
back of her mind, she stepped back into *LA gRANDE SALLE
verte*. Doctor Renard and Doctor Morrisette had obviously just completed a long and exhausting operation
because they were sitting on two straight chairs against
the wall, still in their gear. It struck Agnès they could
also be waiting for the next patient to be wheeled in.
Both men looked worn-down, middle-aged and
stricken, one with his eyes half-closed as if dozing.

A nurse in a long white apron was serving them tea
and biscuits. The slightly taller one was still wearing
his surgical cap, the other had a mass of graying hair
that slinked down his ears. They raised their eyes when
the three women entered.

Abigail took the lead, stepping forward and intro-
ducing them. The doctor with the surgical cap who
grumbled a dissatisfied "Dr Morrisette" inspected
them with a haughty look in his pale blue eyes, but

the gray-haired doctor said with as much cheerfulness as he could muster, "We've been praying for this, Roger. Let's welcome the ladies. Where have you studied?"

"Sorbonne," Agnès and Katell answered at the same time.

Morrisette continued to look skeptical but shook their hands, nonetheless. "André and I are from Lyon," he said in a clipped voice, obviously trying not to seem impressed by their Sorbonne education.

"Never had the pleasure to work with female doctors before but we don't have much to ask for under these circumstances, do we?"

Agnès opened her mouth to protest this discrimination but Renard beat her to it. "Roger, what a rude way to welcome the new doctors," and turning to them, he apologized. "Don't pay any attention to him right now. He's in a bad mood because we couldn't save enough of them poor bastards today. I take it you have experience in the Paris hospitals?"

As Agnès opened her mouth to answer, the door to the operation room swung opened and two carriers jogged in with a heavily bleeding man in a blue uniform.

"Aviation," Morrisette mumbled as he got to his feet.

"You want us to have a look?" Agnès sprang in, already walking towards the cupboard containing the surgical gowns.

"You don't know your way around here," Renard protested, but Katell, following Agnès, said briskly, "We've had to find our way in the American Hospital in

Paris without any doctors and did our jobs there, so it can't be that difficult, gentlemen."

"Please take a break and let us work," Agnès added with determination.

She heard Roger Morrisette mumble, "I may have to change my views about these doctors, but I still think it's a good idea if André and I hang around, just in case."

"No need," Katell chimed in, "we'll ask for you if we need you. Nurse. Cut open his tunic and get the anesthetics ready."

Agnès was surprised to hear the two male doctors leave the room. She eyed Abigail still standing near the door, watching the scene with fascination.

"I can stay, if you want," she offered.

Agnès threw her a grateful smile. "That would be grand. We needed to set out boundaries with those men. Katell and I have had this fight so often in Paris, so we know how to handle it, but we could do with an extra hand and someone to tell where we can find everything. Unless you're too tired?"

"Not at all!" Abigail grinned and her whole face wrinkled up. "I can't think of a better day since I arrived here. I love women power."

With that, the staff of four women put their full concentration on the young aviator on the table.

# 5

## LIVING OR DYING

Agnès and Katell bowed their heads over the patient to inspect his wounds. The young man wore the horizon-blue overalls of the *Armée de l'Air* so was either a French fighter pilot or one of the balloon men, men the air force used to destroy enemy observation balloons. Either way, he'd clearly been catapulted out of his burning plane and had had no time to open his parachute. It was the first time they were treating an airman, as these casualties were too severe to find their way to Paris. A test case for the new doctors, for sure.

Though unconscious and severely maimed, Agnès could not help admiring the strong features of what clearly had been a handsome, daredevil man. Dark eyebrows knitted together above a perfect, strong nose, an exuberant black mustache with dandyish curled tips at the end hid half of his decisive mouth. The firm chin exuded a clear, *Come on, you Bochs, I'll TAKE you down one by one!*

Alas, this time he himself had been at the receiving end of this new phase in warfare. It was a sheer miracle he'd hit the earth the way he had and survived. With burns all over his body, deep head wounds and both his legs broken, Agnès and Katell did not have a second to lose. One of them naturally took the lead and this time it was Katell.

"Give him more oxygen, Abby," she ordered while inspecting his chest and lungs. "He's barely breathing, several ribs broken as well, but we'll come to that later. I'll start with the head wounds. Abby, can you dress the burns on his arms and hands. Agnès, you see to his legs."

The older French nurse who had introduced herself as Clementine rushed to get the trolley with all the equipment the doctors needed.

Agnès frowned. "Right leg is a proper mess, can't set and splint it in any ordinary way. Do you have Thomas splints here, Nurse Clementine?"

Katell looked up from inspecting the pilot's head wounds and shook her head. "You won't have the time for that, Agnès, it's too complicated and will take too long. Look at his condition. He's critical."

"I know. But just in case pilot Pierre Duval makes it, I want him to be able to walk down the aisle to collect his medals once the war is over, instead of being wheeled to the front."

There was stubborn determination in her voice. Thomas splints were incredibly labor-intensive, and she had only assisted another doctor in placing them once. It would mean the constant assistance of one of the nurses, so she frowned, rethinking her options.

"I'll do it anyway, even if it takes me until after dark. Keep me updated on his condition."

Katell shrugged. From the glimpse she'd taken at the pilot's legs, she knew Agnès had made the right diagnosis, but it also meant they would have to sedate him for hours. That had its own risks.

Silence settled on the room as the women worked, the only sounds in the room the faint hissing of the Heidbrink anesthetizer gas machine, the staccato commands of the doctors, and the clacking of the splints being put into place. It was strange, this sudden relative quiet in the huge room where voluptuous angels with harpsichords looked down on the concentrated work under the electric lamps. In the distance the faint boom-boom-boom of cannons bore witness of the perpetual bloodshed that kept them there.

Agnès did not know how many hours they had been standing at the operation table with the only sign of the patient still being alive his shallow but regular breathing.

Finally she exclaimed, "Done!"

"You're amazing." Abigail's voice was full of admiration. "I've only seen this done a couple of times but never so deftly."

Katell had also finished treating the upper part of the patient's body and took a step back. With the back of her hand, she brushed a copper curl aside that had escaped her surgical cap. "I actually think, Major Pierre Duval has a chance at pulling through. If he's lucky he might be up and running within a couple of weeks."

"Well, running," Agnès smirked, "that sounds a little too early, but I agree, he now has a better shot at recovery. Well done, ladies. I think we can go and have some dinner now."

At that moment, the doors to the operation room were pushed open with force and another casualty was brought in.

"Here we go again," Katell observed, rearranging her cap and putting on clean gloves.

Agnès made a strange, almost inhuman sound. It came out as an agonized howl. The patient that was brought in was no other than Jacques. He was lying limply on the stretcher, his skin the color of ashen gray, but seemingly without any wounds.

Restraining herself, she addressed the carrier, "What happened?"

"Shot in the back when he left the car just across from the River Somme. Them damn German snipers," the weary carrier muttered. "I'm so sorry, Doctor, it's the young Count, for sure."

"Get him on the table at once, face down," Agnès ordered and turning to Katell, she added, "Do we notify Elle or look first?"

"Let's look first."

"I agree," Abigail cut in. "Elle's exhausted and there's not much she can do here anyway. Let's get his uniform off."

Without further ado she got out a pair of huge scissors and cut open the rough army-green coat. There was indeed only a small hole in the fabric, no blood. Only one bullet had hit Jacques. But where? It had not come out on the other side, which was not a good sign.

Agnes knew he was critical. His color, the unconsciousness. Her foreboding was right. The bullet had gone through his spine and ripped his spleen but stayed inside. Clean, straight but very damaging. If they managed to get the bullet out, his chances of survival were slim, very slim. And he would always be paralyzed because it had hit at T12, a sure place for a transverse lesion. Even so, the damage to his organs would be a greater threat. As long as the bullet was inside, it was a time bomb.

"Turn him over. We have to work from the front."

"Let me do the operation, Agnès," Katell insisted.

"We'll need to cut open his entire belly, from his midriff down and I'm the only one who's done a similar operation in Paris. And in case he dies, you'll not have to carry the blame for it."

"You can be head surgeon but I'm here to assist," Agnès said defiantly. "Only for medical clarity I assent to you taking the lead. None other."

Knowing her friend's ethics when it came to her profession, Katell wisely said no more.

"We are here, too," Abby said. "We'll do what we can."

"Scalpel," Katell ordered, and the operation was under way.

As always time fell away when Agnès was at the operation table. Tiredness and emotions had no place anymore. Vaguely she was aware that the light outside had faded into a blurry black but only when Katell said, "Multi-layered stitching can begin," did she feel some form of empty relief. They had been able to remove the bullet and stop further internal bleeding, but his spleen was perforated, and the damage was considerable, as was blood loss during the operation.

For the next day or two Jacques would be hovering between life and death.

"Time to let Elle know," Abigail said, "unless you need me here?"

"No, I can clean up," Nurse Clementine replied. "You go break the news."

"I really hope we can get some dinner inside us now," Katell sighed. "It's strange how these long operations always seem to give me appetite." She stopped talking in her upbeat tone when she saw how Agnès's gaze rested on the sleeping Jacques. "You okay, *chérie*?"

Agnès nodded. "It's not that he was even my friend, but I must say that after this short reintroduction, it really upsets me to see him like this. I'm kind of fond of him, you know." She folded Jacques' silver- rimmed glasses that had been lying on the side table and absentmindedly put them in the pocket of her doctor's coat. "Look at him, in the prime of his life, not even a soldier and a stray bullet may have ended it all for him."

"Be optimistic, Agnès; he's strong and we did what we could. Nurse and I will wheel him into the recovery room now. Someone has to stay with him for the next couple of hours and make sure he remains heavily sedated. The pain will be excruciating when he wakes up. Stomach wounds are the worst."

As if called by a bell the two male doctors returned to the operation room. After giving their colleagues an update on the two severe cases they'd had to handle in the past hours, the women took their leave.

"We'll pop in later to look into the pilot and the Count," Agnès promised.

She was glad to leave that opulent room where they might or might not have saved two more lives, but her shoulders hung as she made her way back to the garden room, mentally bracing for the accusing eyes of Elle on her.

~

CONTRARY TO HER EXPECTATION, she found Elle in tears, hanging onto Abigail and howling like a wounded animal.

"I should have gone myself. My eyesight is much better than Jacques's. I would have ducked. The bastards! The bastards."

She looked up when Agnès and Katell reluctantly entered the room, ready to give the grieving sibling some time alone if needed. But the topaz eyes lit up on seeing them.

"Thank you so much, Agnès and Kat, you're wonderful! Truly wonderful! I'm actually glad you two operated on Jacques and not these ghastly Lyon doctors. They may be good at what they do but I don't like them one bit. So condescending and superior all the time."

"We don't know if he'll make it, Elle," Katell said prudently, making sure she kept her friend out of the wind. "Your brother's severely wounded. We also have no idea if he'll ever be able to walk again. It may have been a stray bullet, but it hit him in the wrong place."

"When will we know?" Elle sat up straight, looking a little more combative than before.

"We'll probably know in the next day or two.

Tonight is especially critical. And then we hope there aren't any complications, like festering wounds or high fevers. Whether he will be able to walk again, will take a little longer. When he's conscious, we'll ask him what he can feel in his lower body, but it can be weeks before we're certain."

"I'm going to sit next to his bed all night," Elle declared, already getting up from her chair.

"No, you're not," Abigail forbade. "At this moment you can do nothing at all because he's asleep. Later we'll take it in turns. Now we all need rest and have a bite to eat."

THE NIGHT TURNED OUT TO be a long and pitiful one. Both Jacques and the pilot remained steady for the rest of the evening but when Agnès's head finally hit her pillow, she couldn't sleep. Not only the war seemed to come closer and closer, the extreme tiredness of her body and mind forbade her rest. She was wide awake, listening to Katell's even breathing in the other bed. Part of her anxiety was due to finding herself in the same bedroom she had stayed in with Gåva nine years earlier.

Finally, at four in the morning, she gave in and slipped out of bed. On tiptoe and only with her dressing gown over her nightdress and in a pair of old shoes, she entered the recovery ward to check on the pilot and Jacques.

They were sleeping side by side with a stout nurse nodding in between the two silent beds. All seemed normal but Agnès's instinct told her it wasn't. The pilot was alright although cringing with pain despite his sedation, but Jacques lay too peaceful, too far gone. She wondered whether she should wake Elle or Katell but for some reason she was unable to move from her place, her feet in their old shoes glued to the floor, her hand resting on his shallow pulse.

The nurse snored softly and the incessant growl of the war outside rattled her nerves. It intensified when a squadron of airplanes roared overhead, either Allied bombers or German ones. No alarm went off, so she remained where she was, realizing that she could be killed on the spot in a matter of seconds.

Agnès didn't even feel the cold as she sat down at the other side of Jacques' bed. The shimmering light of one candle lit up his dark features, now hollow and eerily still. At some point she started to breathe in Jacques's rhythm as if her breath would help steady his and pull him through.

Flashes of him as an adolescent, fixing her with that intense gaze from under a dark lock of hair, a stunningly beautiful face, exploring her eyes, probing her soul. She knew him and she didn't. Even now lying still on the brink of death, he confused her, especially because he had put his life in her hands. Without knowing where it came from, Solveig's Song drifted to her and Agnès found herself singing the words as if in a trance.

*The winter MAY PASS AND the spring DISAPPEAR, the summer too will VANISH AND then the yEAR.*

*But this I know for CERTAIN: thou'lt come BACK AGAIN; And*
*e'en AS I promised, thou'lt find me WAITING then. God help*
*thee, when WAND'RING thy WAY ALL ALONe,*
*God grANT thee his strength AS thou kneel'st AT his throne.*
*If thou now ART WAITING in hEAV'N for me,*
*O there we'll meet AGAIN love AND never PARTED be!*

"DON'T DIE, JACQUES," she prayed, "don't die on me." It didn't even matter now that she couldn't hold her tune. Papa would forgive her and the nurse slept on. So she sang it again, now in Norwegian, first a little rusty and then purer, with more confidence.

Another flash of memory passed through her. First, she didn't know whence it came, a woman with long gold hair and heavenly blue eyes, beautiful as the Virgin Mary herself. But this angel was rocking her and singing the same words as a lullaby.

Agnès's eyes filled with tears. "Mother?" she asked in the night. "Mother, are you there?"

Afraid she was losing her mind, Agnès forced herself to get up and inspect the pilot's dressings, then monitoring Jacques's morphine dose. Anything to shut out the eerie thoughts.

It was getting really cold around her now and she knew she had to leave Jacques and go back into bed. She turned and from the corner of her eye she saw Jacques stir. Stepping back quickly into the flickering light, she gazed intently into his face. His eyelids were open, but he wasn't seeing anything.

"Jacques," she whispered, waving her fingers before his eyes for a reaction. "Jacques are you there?"

Nothing happened. *This is it*, she thought. She'd

seen this kind of semi-awaking so often. The last reflex, before death. It took her breath away, every time.

So she couldn't believe what she saw when he slowly turned his face in her direction, trying to focus his gaze. It wasn't death, it was something else. His eyelids fell over the tired eyes again but then he moved his mouth. No sound came out as his tongue was glued to his pallet.

"Wait, let me get you some water."

Agnès held the glass with the straw to his mouth and to her surprise he sucked and took a small sip. He opened his eyes again, trying to find her face. Her heart jumped, this was a miracle, but the doctor in her knew he didn't understand what had happened to him. It was her task to tell him in small portions what had taken place. This was a crucial but cruel part of her job. Clarity above all else. She took her seat again and taking his hand in hers explained in simple words what she knew about his accident and what she and Katell had to do. She had no idea how much he absorbed.

"Agnès," he croaked, and kept repeating her name. "Agnès, Agnès."

That was the moment she knew he had a chance to live. He might be a cripple, but he had a chance.

## 6

## RECOVERY

*Château de Dragancourt, August 1917*

THE SUNLIGHT FILTERED through the gauze curtains, shedding a golden aureole on Agnes's fair head. She sat on the sofa in the garden room, taking a short break from her early morning shift, enjoying a cup of coffee and a ham sandwich. It was exceptional to be in the room on her own for a quiet moment.

Ever since she and Katell had arrived at Dragancourt five weeks earlier, the garden room had always been a beehive, night and day. Staff and drivers, castle personnel and the occasional Allied major, would drop in for a coffee, a chat and a smoke.

Agnès needed this moment of peace and quiet to calm her tired brain and body. Though she had come a long way from her introverted girlhood, the hectic and strenuous life in the warzone hospital was taking its toll.

She and Katell had not had time to evaluate their sudden jump from Paris to the frontlines but both knew that what they were doing was urgent and unstoppable, saving as many lives as possible. They continued day in day out without taking a break.

In this rare tranquil moment, the weeks flashed by and Agnès felt many conflicting emotions. Most of all she missed her father, his voice, his smell, his embrace. In all her young life he alone had been the pivotal person, the one she could turn to, build her world on. She had soldiered on bravely after he was stuck in Sweden for the duration of the war, pushing the thought of him to the back of her mind, but on this sunny morning in mid-August, with cannons booming and wounded men crying out in agony, she longed for her Papa with every fiber of her being. No word had come from Sweden for months, despite her weekly letters, and she wondered if he even knew where she was.

"Of course, he does," she corrected herself. "He

used to phone every fortnight, so Mrs. Proulx will have told him. I just have to be patient and endure. Papa will come back when the war is over. When the war is over," Agnès repeated before returning her attention to her current life at Dragancourt.

The relationship with Elle was friendly but strained. Of course, Elle understood she and Katell were in no way to blame for Jacques's accident and subsequent paralysis, but as his breakdown had coincided with their arrival, somehow these two events had blended in Elle's mind. She wasn't hostile, she was absent. Elle had shrunk, become quiet and withdrawn.

The only times she talked were with Abby. Next to that she did her shifts, working even harder than before.

Agnès now understood - more so than when she'd been in their orbit the first time - that Elle and Jacques were two sides of the same coin. They were twin souls, and one could not properly function without the other. Often, she would find Elle sitting silently by her brother's bed, not talking, her mind miles away, an unhappy frown between the magnificent eyes.

Everybody tried to help Elle but stubborn and strong as she was, she sulked on her own and took up Jacques's managing tasks on top of her shifts.

Jacques, Agnès had come to understand, had been the main manager of the operation, creating the schedules for the doctors, nurses and drivers. He had made the lists for stocks that were needed both food-wise and for the hospital, so a huge vacuum had been created with him being incapacitated. Nobody could really replace Jacques, as he had been the right hand man. Now everybody tried to do their bit, but the machine didn't run as smoothly as it had done before.

Also, the relationship between the two male doctors and the newcomers remained tense. Morrisette in particular continued to have a grudge against female physicians and every soldier that died at Agnès's or Katell's hands seemed to weigh heavier than his own mortal cases.

Agnès sighed and momentarily closed her eyes. It was all so much to take in and the only light spot in it all - apart from Katell's presence - was the fact that Jacques was slowly but certainly on the mend. The transverse lesion had not been a total rupture after all.

All the medical staff were holding their breath but there was a glimmer of hope that he would be able to learn to walk again.

Despite the good news, Agnès was always apprehensive to go into his sick room. Whenever possible she let one the other doctors tend to him. Jacques took it hard, his invalid status, so his moodiness and restlessness got to her every time. She'd done what she could but maybe it hadn't been enough, or a more practiced surgeon would have approached the operation differently.

"We have to find a way of getting him to Papa in London," Elle had said one night at dinner.

"That would indeed be the best for him," Agnès had agreed. "He feels useless here and we also cannot offer him the rehabilitation he needs."

Jacques wouldn't hear of it; despite the absence of a physical therapist and despite the threat of the war closing in by the day, he insisted on staying at Dragancourt.

"At least I'll be able to help from my bed soon," he protested, "and I don't want to be packed off to another country. I want to be right here when we finally beat the Boches and France is once again ours."

For the time being Jacques stayed where he was. Guillaume had created a room for him downstairs, adjacent to the garden room, so the patient only needed to ring his bedside bell, and someone would pop a head around the door to see to his needs.

At that very moment Agnès heard the high tingling of the little bell in Jacques' room. She got up, straightened her doctor's coat and slowly made her way through the door.

Jacques had been reading Siegfried Sassoon's war poems, the book with the poet's clean-shaven, friendly face staring at her as it lay open on his stomach. When he turned his dark eyes to Agnès, she saw he was moved by the words he'd read, and she braced herself. At times, it was such a difficult equilibrium, being a physician and a friend.

"How are you feeling?" Though a standard question, she knew just how to put the right amount of warmth in it.

"Bloody awful." It was neither accusatory, nor complaining. A statement, but one full of feeling. "I wasn't created to be an invalid. I was always the sportsman, you know, but now I can only see my body walk and run and row or swim in my mind's eye. It's sheer agony. Will I ever be able to get up again, Agnès?"

She sat on the chair next to his bed, folding her hands in her lap. "I don't know. I know that's not the answer you want but it's all I've got."

"Nobody understands what I'm going through." It sounded so desolate.

"I think I both can and I can't," she offered. "I've never been keen on sports myself, apart from a little horse riding, so I can't really say what it is like for you, but I do get that taking any faculty away is a hard thing to adapt to. I would be very angry and upset myself."

Jacques fixed her with the somber gaze. "Well, here I am lamenting my fate when I haven't even properly thanked you for saving my life. Sorry for my ungratefulness. Without you and Kat I wouldn't even be alive."

Agnès laughed cheerlessly. "Don't say that, Jacques. You underestimate the Lyon doctors. They're taking excellent care of you as well and if they had operated on you, they may have even done a better job, who knows?"

"We'll never know," he remarked gruffly, "but what I do know is that the death rate here at Dragan- court has gone down since you two arrived. Now it could be that the casualties are less severe, but I wouldn't know why that would be the case."

"Jacques!" she cried out. "Don't tell me you've been working. I expressly instructed Elle not to give you any information."

"You may have impressed her with your plea but don't underestimate Guillaume," Jacques grinned. It was nice seeing him smile again. "But don't worry, I've only been doing a little managing from my sickbed for the last couple of days."

Agnès's blue eyes bored into his. "As your doctor, if I had known, I would've have forbidden you. Not only your body needs rest, so does your mind. Healing is a process, not just the injured parts must rest, all of you must rest for the best possible result."

"Ha," he scoffed, "and what if working helps me heal? Just lying here all day makes me miserable and depressed, so I see no harm in it."

"Let me have a look at your reflexes." Agnès ignored this last remark. "Any feeling in the legs?"

"Not much, but I thought I felt a tremor in my right leg last night."

"Really?" Agnès cheered. "That's great news, Jacques! That's the beginning."

"The beginning of what?"

"Of functions starting to get back. Let me see." She pulled the blanket off him and pushed hard on the sole of his feet.

"Feel anything?"

"I wish I did," he smirked, "it's not every day that a pretty doctor touches my feet."

"Oh, you," she laughed and slapped his ankle.

"Ouch!" he said.

"What? Did you feel that?"

"That you slapped my ankle? Yes." Tears sprang into Agnès's eyes, which made Jacques ask in a worried voice, "What's wrong, Agnès?"

"It means ... Jacques, it means that you will walk. One day you'll walk again." Agnès couldn't control herself and started sobbing, while Jacques's eyes grew large as life.

"Walk," he repeated. "Walk." As if it was a word in a foreign tongue. But then he collected himself, understanding hers were tears of joy. He added in a tender tone, "Come here, let me give you a hug. You're a miracle, Doctor Agnès, you're *my* miracle."

Before she knew what was happening, he had pulled her in his strong arms, causing her to land half on his chest.

"Thank you," he murmured in her hair.

Agnès pulled herself up to look into his eyes. There were tears in his eyes and it made her feel vulnerable. She'd seen many male patients cry for various reasons but never one she knew so well. This strong man was shedding tears because he would walk again. Before she could say anything, he pulled her tighter against him and for a moment she let him. They lay quietly together until the strong emotions subsided.

His heartbeat under his pajama jacket against her doctor's coat felt so normal though it was the opposite of normal.

"My life saver." He kissed the top of her head. "My second-time life saver."

Agnès did not want to break the warm bond she felt at that moment; while still lying against his chest, she asked, "What do you mean? The second time?"

"The first time was nine years ago. You do not know this but when I left you on that drawbridge that led to your father's castle, I vowed I would never deliberately mock or hurt another being again. We did you wrong, Agnès, both Elle and I."

She felt his chest expand as he took a deep breath. "We don't deserve your sympathy after the inhospitable reception you had here as a young lady. I figured that out there and then. After I dropped you off, I asked my father permission to travel abroad, just to get my head square on my shoulders again. I traveled for almost two years, Africa, India and even six months through Australia. But at some point, I knew I wasn't going to make a difference traveling by myself and enjoying the different cultures and sights. It was just another way of indulging in luxury."

He took another breath and continued, "While I was crossing from continent to continent, I started writing. So on my return to London, I set out to find a publisher and that's how I published my first book, *Travels Through No Man's Land*. Strangely enough, that book brought me closer to you. I always remembered the way your face lit up when you talked about Henry James's novels. How you loved books, the thin string we shared. I even played with the idea to dedicate the book to you."

Agnès unwrapped herself from his embrace now to look at him. "You wrote a book? And you wanted to dedicate it to me? Why? We never saw each other again."

"I know. And I know it sounds weird when I admit you'd gotten under my skin, right from the first time we met. Of course, I played the rogue part to perfection, but I jolly well knew I was doing it because you confused me so deeply. I'd never come across someone with your purity, your innocence, your loveliness. I just didn't know how to handle it. And I think neither did Elle."

"Stop it, Jacques," Agnès smiled. "I'm no saint. Far from it. Ask Katell. I'm a gritty lady, she would say."

"Whatever," Jacques shrugged, "as long as you know all those years it was you who propelled me forwards. So I tried to be good, to do good, to help others along the way, to always see the beauty in things. All I had seen in you."

He swallowed and Agnès saw he was sincere. His words broke through the ring of hardness she'd had to create around her own heart so as not to feel, to be able to go on and do her job.

Jacques wouldn't stop now. "When the war broke out, I didn't doubt two seconds to ask my father to turn Dragancourt into a war hospital. I didn't know how long we'd be on the frontlines and couldn't have fathomed it was ... is already three years now. One day blurred into another and even your image dissipated at times." He had the exact look he's seen on his face when he approached then in LA GRANDE SALLE *verte* five weeks earlier. "So when you walked into my castle, I thought it was you in the form of an angel. Never in my boldest dreams would I've dared to dream you'd ever come back. But you did."

The look he gave her now melted right into her heart.

"I don't know how to respond to this." She started plucking nervously on one of the buttons on her doctor's coat. "I really don't."

"Oh, I understand that alright." Jacques lit a cigarette with an irritated movement. "People fall for other people every day all over the globe and the other half never knows, never realizes the intense yearning it causes."

"What do you mean?" The question was unnecessary, the pain was all over his face. "Jacques," she said softly, "don't."

"So, there's someone else?" He took a long draw on his cigarette.

"No! I don't mean that. I mean, I mean ..." She stared out of the window with a mist before her eyes, unable to face him. This man was her patient, the rules were very clear, but he certainly created a tangle in her emotions.

At that moment she heard the door to the garden room being opened and Katell's voice calling, "Anybody here? Agnès? Can you help?"

She shot up, "I have to go. I'll check in later.

Anything you need?"

The dark eyes went right through her soul as he said with intense melancholy, "No. I'll be alright. Please forget this conversation, Agnès. The last thing I want is to be a burden to you."

"You're not a burden, Jacques. You move me." She lay a soft hand on his immovable leg and gave it a little squeeze.

His eyes laughed through the pain as he uttered, "Ouch."

## 7

## ONE AND THE SAME GIRL

That evening a rather flushed Agnès sat down to the dinner table with Elle, Katell and the rest of the medical staff. She was glad everybody was too tired and cooped up in their own thoughts to pay much attention to her, but she felt Katell's eyes on her a couple of times and knew she would demand an explanation for her red cheeks later. But though flustered and shaky, the professional won in Agnès as always.

After they had finished a watery soup of cabbage and leeks with the tiniest bit of minced meat in it, she turned to Elle and said, "Jacques has feeling in his shins. This means that the lesion is not complete. Now we really need to get him out of here and onto a recovery program. We'd be doing him a great disfavor by keeping him here. I hope you see my point."

Elle looked up from her unfinished soup terrain and lit a cigarette. "But that's great news, isn't it?" she said hesitantly.

"It is."

"Why didn't you tell us straightaway?" Katell broke in.

Agnès smiled. "I wanted everyone to quench their hunger first because I knew there would be tons of questions if I brought it up immediately.

"I'm never hungry these days anyway," Elle observed, taking another drag on her cigarette.

"But you have to try," Agnès spurred her. "I've been watching you, Elle, and you really need to eat more."

"Maybe I can now," she shrugged, "now I know my brother has a chance of being a fully functioning human being again."

"So how shall we go about it?" Agnès asked. "Who do you think would have the most convincing power over Jacques? Because it's clear he doesn't want to leave Dragancourt."

A silence followed and then all the women around the table pointed to her. "You."

"Me?" Agnès looked doubtful.

to you if you explain to him that this is his only chance at some kind of a normal life."

Agnès sighed. This was the last task on earth she was looking forward to.

"I agree," Elle said through her smoke. "He'll never listen to his sister, though I'm ten minutes older than he is, and the rest of the staff has no influence whatsoever. He likes you and in the end he'll listen."

There seemed no way around it, so she consented. "Just let me do it tomorrow, not tonight. He'll be tired and recalcitrant. I'll talk to him in the morning."

After dinner Katell immediately came over to Agnès. "Let's go outside where the walls have no ears. I want to hear it all."

"Hear what?"

"You know. The rest of it. You're hiding something from me."

"No, I'm not," Agnes blushed.

They went through the open doors of the garden room and stepped into the sultry August evening. The hortensias and buddleias spread their heavy scent and momentarily pushed the smell of rubber and smoke aside that normally permeated the air.

"Gosh, one could say it's even lovely for a moment," Katell inhaled, "if you could put your fingers in your ears and forget the noise this war makes."

On this side of the castle there were no patients, no ambulances and no staff, just the sloping *jardin à la Francaise* and the drone of the war to the north east.

Agnès put her arm through Katell's and they sauntered over to one of the benches under the rose arch and sat down.

"How have you been?" Agnès had not seen her friend all day as they had agreed to spend the day each working with the male doctors in an attempt to improve their mutual relationships.

"You mean with Roger?" Katell grinned.

"Oh, are you on familiar terms with him now?

That's an improvement, I guess."

"Depends how you look at it. His bite is not as bad as his bark, you could say. And he's an excellent surgeon, taught me a difficult dental operation today.

Restructuring a jaw isn't easy. So yes, I think it worked. I mean, we've been here for almost two months now and I'm not one to work well when there's not really a team spirit."

"I know what you mean, "Agnès agreed. "Renard wasn't as bad either, but I still prefer to work with you. It's not so much that he isn't good, it's just that we're so well adjusted to each other. I only need half a word to know what you need, whereas with him it's not as natural."

"So it will be you and me again tomorrow?"

"Yes," Agnès answered, "we can do some shifts with the men, but I prefer to stay close to you. You always make my work better."

"You're a sweet one," Katell squeezed her hand, "but now tell me what happened between you and Jacques."

"Why do you suppose something happened?" Agnès tried to buy time. Her feelings were still so confused about the sudden intimacy they had shared and all his passionate words, she wasn't even sure she could put any of it in words right now.

"Oh, come on, Aggie, I know you like the inside of my pocket. Did he kiss you?"

"No!" But she knew it was a white lie. Jacques had kissed the top of her head, next to all the sweet words he'd uttered. All of it made her heart flutter and her limbs shake.

"Well, something happened or you wouldn't color the way you do every time someone mentions his name."

Katell fixed her with the green stare and for some

reason, Agnès needed her friend closer so crept towards her and leaned into her.

"He confuses me," she confessed. "I don't know what he wants from me and that confuses me. I'm his doctor, Kat, he's my patient. You know what that means."

Katell put her arm around her shoulder and drew her even closer. "That's of no consequence here, Aggie. Everyone with eyes can see Jacques likes you, he likes you very much and that's why you have to use that power over him to convince him he has to leave Dragancourt and get the help he needs."

Agnès nodded. "I will. But I think I will miss him." "Of course, you will. We will all miss him. Jacques is the spin in the web. He breathes Dragancourt and this frontline hospital. But we'll manage without him and have to keep praying this awful war will be over soon and we can all go home."

"Why are you always so level-headed, Kat? I don't know what I'd do without you."

"Thank you, Aggie, and we do this together, remember. We always did and we always will." A silence followed, after which Katell said in no more than a whisper, "Give it time, Aggie, let him go now. See how you feel about him. See what happens to him. He might still change his mind. This is not the time to make important decisions."

"Maybe it is, maybe it isn't, but the doctor in me knows what I have to do."

"I'm so sorry," Katell added, "even with my wicked sense of humor I don't want to make this lighter for you. It doesn't seem appropriate. Let me just say I'm vouching for the two of you."

WITH A HEAVY HEART Agnès went into Jacques's room the next morning. She found him absorbed in his clipping board, his glasses halfway down the bridge of his nose, a pencil between his lips. He smiled as he looked up and she saw the news of his possible recovery had lifted his spirits.

"Ah," he exclaimed, "my favorite doctor. How good of you to come and see your invalid."

"Don't say that. The end of this is around the corner but only if you listen to me."

"Are we being stern today?" he joked but the cautiousness in her eyes silenced him. "Sorry, Agnès, what is it that you came to say?"

She took down the bed clothes and checked his reflexes again. Same as yesterday. Hopeful but far from perfect.

"Jacques," she began solemnly, "I need you to listen very carefully and open-mindedly to me. Can you do that?"

"Oh God, what have I done wrong now?" He threw his arms into the air in despair.

"No, you haven't done anything wrong. But I need to broach something that I know you don't want to hear."

"Like leaving Dragancourt? No way." He stuck out his chin like a defiant little boy.

"Yes, like leaving Dragancourt. But listen before you

raise your hackles, okay? Elle has asked me to bring this up with you because she's sure you wouldn't listen to her. And the other doctors agree with me as well. Your only chance at a normal life after the war is if you agree to go to a convalescent center. If you don't want to go to England, at least go to Paris. I know a renowned institute there where they can develop a custom-made program for you to train your muscles every day. You might be able to walk again in six to eight months."

While she kept talking, her blue eyes were steady, not betraying her thumping heart. She saw she had his full attention, but he was still shaking his head.

"You have to think of yourself now, Jacques. What use will you be to yourself or others if you throw away this chance just to do some management jobs here at the front?" She stopped again, pleading with him.

"I can't go without you, Agnès. I need to be near you every day and I know you want to stay here, so I'm torn. I do get what you say but what if I leave and you find someone else ..." His voice trailed off.

Agnès stood up straighter and though befuddled and flushed, said angrily, "Jacques, don't! As if I have time to think of my love life in this situation. I'm not like you."

His face dropped as if she had slapped him, and she instantly regretted her harsh words.

"Sorry, I shouldn't have. I'm tired," she excused herself.

He turned away from her and, staring out of the window, started citing in a low voice "'*They HAD found themselves looking AT EACh other straight, AND for A longer time on end THAN WAS USUAL even AT PARTIES in GALLERIES;*

but THAT, AFTER ALL, *would* HAVE *been* A SMALL *Affair, if there* HADN'T *been something else with it. It* WASN'T, IN A *word, simply* THAT *their eyes* HAD *met; other conscious organs, faculties, feelers* HAD *met* AS *well.*'"

This was such an unexpected turn of events that Agnès had to sit down. "*The Wings of the Dove*," she whispered. "You remember?"

"Of course, I do. How couldn't I? And I listen, too!" Jacques threw his arms in the air as a sign of resignation. It *WAS* after all only their eyes that could meet at this moment in time.

Agnès felt her heart contract but with a glimmer of hope. He would go, he'd said as much and then ... then they would see. Get through this bloody war first. No promises, no expectations, just survival.

"So you'll go?" It was asked ever so softly. She thought he'd not even heard her, but he nodded.

"On one condition." "Being?"

"That you'll save the first liberation dance for me." The mischievous, dark glint was back in his eyes and Agnès felt herself drawn to him as metal powder to a magnet.

"Promise!" Her smile was happy. Maybe they would all win.

"See you in Paris then." His words were simple but warm.

"I'll be there. It's just that the Germans are setting the date, not us."

⁓

THAT EVENING AGNÈS lay in bed, on the one side relieved that Jacques had agreed to find treatment in Paris, on the other hand sad that this confusing attraction was coming to an end.

*Am I in love?* the dreamer in her pondered. And she fell asleep, feeling as one person again after a very long time. The socially awkward bookish fifteen-year-old and the decisive, professional doctor. One and the same girl.

## 8

## THE END OF THE WAR

*Dragoncourt, 11 November 1918*

The steward Guillaume came rushing into the operation room, his face flushed and the lapels of his coat flapping behind him.

Agnès and Katell were helping a gassed American soldier who had difficulty breathing, annoyance in their eyes at the disruption. Despite the urgency that often reigned in LA GRANDE SALLE *verte*, there were strict protocols around who entered and who didn't, which meant no entrance for staff that had no use to be there.

But before Agnès could protest, Guillaume cried out, "The war is over, the war is over!" Jubilantly he threw his chauffeur's cap into the air.

Agnès and Katell looked from him to each other in disbelief. There had been so many moments in the past months that the Allied forces had been close, breaking through the Hindenburg line at Montdidier and Verdun. The German general Ludendorff seemed to have almost given up and there were so many rumors of enemy soldiers surrendering by the thousands. But still, the summer had turned to fall, and the cold weather had set in. Despite huge losses, the Germans had stood their ground.

"Is it true?" Agnès asked, her surgical glove resting of the American's arm as if giving him strength.

At that moment Elle and Abby rushed in as well. "War is over, the Germans capitulated."

Then they were all hugging each other, tears streaming down their cheeks. The four-year horror had finally, *fINALLY* come to an end, four long years of fear and death, of lack of everything. It was too big to grasp. Agnès had to sit down on a chair in the operation room and let her tears take their spill. Papa could finally come home, she and Katell could return to Paris, they could build up their lives again.

"You're okay?" Katell sank down on the chair next to her. "You know we have to finish giving Peter Swift more air? We can't leave the poor man lying there gasping for oxygen."

"I know, just give me a minute. I'll recover."

They quickly put the American on the incubator and he came by again, his hazel eyes wide with wonder.

"The war is over," they told him, and he smiled despite the contraption over his mouth, tears sliding down the side of his temples.

"God bless," were the words his mouth formed, and his fingers made the V sign.

"You're hopefully our very last patient, Corporal Swift," Katell told him, taking off her gown and snapping off the surgical mask. "Thank God, we have no worries that you'll make it and will get back to your family. So many of your fellow men died under our hands."

"But many more survived, though many will also be maimed for life," Agnès added, and her thoughts went to Jacques.

They had had regular updates on his progress, and he seemed to be doing well.

The American made a sign that he wanted to breath independently for a moment, so they took the tube from his mouth.

"Thank you, doctors," he croaked. "I'm from Austin, Texas, and I hope to return there soon. Then I want to live to a ripe old age, so I'll always remember these two angels on the French frontlines fighting as hard as the men in the trenches. I'll tell the story of Doctor de Melancourt and Doctor Katell to my grandchildren and make sure they listen to it with their ears open."

"Thank you," they said in unison, moved by the force of this statement. They knew he would. Their work had not been for naught.

After Swift was wheeled out of the operation room and the doctors had checked on the patients that were still in the ward, Elle assembled them all in the garden room.

"There will still be some rounding off to do here but I truly believe two doctors and half of the nurses will be enough," she began.

Agnès observed how thin and tired Elle looked and thought she needed a break as well.

"We'll stay on for a while, Elle," she interrupted.

"Why don't you take a few days to be with Jacques in Paris. It'll do you good."

On mentioning her brother's name, Elle seemed to revive.

"Could I?" But then her delight seemed to evaporate. "No, I can't." She shook her dark head. "It's very likely that the French authorities will come to take stock now, to see who's still here. We also may have to house a regiment of Allied soldiers before they return to their home countries. I can't be missed."

"Who can't be missed?" All faces looked up as Jacques, between two crutches, stood in the doorway.

"Jacques!" Elle cried. "Brother, is it really you?"

She flung herself at him and Jacques was almost thrown off balance, forcing Elle to keep him upright in her muscled arms. All that stretcher bearing had made her immensely strong despite being underweight.

The intense happiness of the twin's reunion was deeply moving to all of them. Jacques was standing and the war was over.

AN HOUR later as Jacques sat in their midst in his father's chair, and tea and biscuits were being handed around, Agnès was aware of a strange tightness in her chest. Jacques seemed changed; all the former restlessness had gone from him. He sat as if he presided over the room, calm and content, his brown eyes glistening behind the round glasses. Now and then he glanced in her direction, but he was mainly occupied with answering Elle's numerous questions. She had positioned herself on the arm of his chair and would not budge from his side. With Jacques back, Elle de Dragancourt was finally at peace.

"I had a phone call from Father this morning," Agnès heard Jacques say. "He'll be coming over as soon as the ferries between England and France are restored."

FATHer, Agnès thought. Her father would be able to return to Paris now as well.

As if she had evoked a higher power, Guillaume stuck his head around the door. "Phone call from Sweden for Doctor de Melancourt."

She rose from her chair and felt all the emotions of the past years go through her, such a heavy weight, so many events, and all without her beloved parent.

"Papa," she wailed into the mouthpiece, unable to control herself any longer, "Papa!"

"Oh, my dear one, my little dear one," she heard his familiar voice in her ear and was soothed instantly. "How are you, my dear dapper daughter? Elise and I and the children will be on the first boat that sails from Malmö, I can guarantee you."

"When do you think that will be, Papa? I miss you so much."

"I've been on the phone with the shipping company all morning and it seems we'll be able to obtain tickets for the end of this month. With a bit of luck, we'll be home from Christmas."

As she talked to her father, trying to feel him near her as best as she could, Agnès sensed someone was standing behind her. She turned her head. It was

Jacques with his finger to his lips, leaning on his crutches.

After she'd said goodbye to her father, he asked, "Can we find a quiet place where we can chat?" His eyes found hers.

"Sure." Agnès still in her doctor's coat accompanied him to the room that had been used as Jacques' recovery room after the accident. It had not really been used since he'd left in the summer of 1917, and Agnès took down the furniture coverings so they could sit down. Both were silent.

"How are you?" she ventured.

"I'm good," he smiled. "You did the right thing sending me away. I've been focusing on my recovery, read a lot and thought a lot."

"Glad to hear it. What did you think about?" It seemed an innocent question but Agnès was aware of the meaning behind it.

"Everything under the sun, but a lot about you as well."

"About me?" Agnès stared down on her slim, surgeon's fingers, feeling apprehensive. So much was happening in such a short time.

"Yes, I really had to curb my whimsical self a minute ago. I almost wanted to grab that receiver from you and talk to your dad."

Agnès raised her blue gaze to his, her heart beating wildly. "You wanted to do what?"

She sounded angrier than she meant to, so he quickly added, "Yes, I know, I'm incorrigible. I thought I had become so balanced and mature in my recovery year, but one look at you and immediately I'm my old devilish self again. I'll never stand a chance with you. I know that now."

The sadness in his voice touched her but his rude overruling of her feelings still lingered.

"Sorry, "he said softly, "you must be at the end of your tether and here I come barging in talking about reading books and time to think. It's impertinent of me not to ask after your well-being. I've had all the leisure in the world while you and Elle and Katell and the rest of them worked your socks off here."

"It's okay, Jacques. We're so glad you're here. We've missed you. Dragancourt is not the same without you."

"Do you mean that, Agnès?" "I do."

"So you and Katell will leave for Paris soon, won't you?"

"Yes, as soon as the last patients can be transported, we'll take our leave."

"What will you do?" There was an eagerness in his voice.

She thought for a moment. "Take a break, maybe go to our house in Nice until Father returns to Paris. Just a change of scenery. Make up my mind what to do next. This war has stolen so much from us, not only a couple of years. We've become old before we realized it."

"You're not old! I am. I will be thirty next spring." Jacques still held her gaze in his. Much remained unspoken between them. "I don't dare to take one more step in your direction, Agnès." Jacques lit a cigarette, still studying her through the smoke. "By God, I wished I knew how to make up for all my blunders."

"It's not you, Jacques." It came out hesitantly. "It's

me. I know how to be a daughter. I know how to be a doctor. I just don't know how to be a woman."

To her surprise he burst out laughing, but not in a mean way. "You? Not a woman? I know no one who is more feminine than you, my dear Agnès. You ARe the embodiment of femininity."

She frowned. "Really? Uhm." She looked terribly young and vulnerable as she said that.

"Would you ... would you ever dare to take a chance on an imperfect man such as me?"

The golden sunlight filled the room in the antique castle that had sighed under the war but had never surrendered. Agnès sat very still, thinking and feeling too much for her slender frame.

Finally, she nodded, her face a portrait of bliss and joy. "I think I will."

"Come here," Jacques beckoned her.

She went to him and sat on the arm of his chair, as she had seen Elle doing so often. But he pulled her in his lap, cupping her chin to make their eyes meet. He looked so in love, such masculine beauty. She soaked up all of him, his intensity, his warmth, his unfailing commitment to her.

"Will you do me the honor of becoming my wife, Agnès Gunárssón?"

It was her signal to act. Throwing all her caution overboard, she didn't answer but kissed him with a ferocity he'd clearly not expected.

"I guess, that's a *yes*?" he gasped in between kisses.

"It's a MAYbe," Agnès teased.

"Let's go and tell the others!" Jacques's happiness clearly knew no boundaries anymore.

Hand in hand they entered the garden room. They all seemed to know. Both Kat and Elle had tears of joy in their eyes. At that moment Agnès knew it had been Jacques all along.

Ever since she was fifteen.

# EPILOGUE

## A CHANGE OF HEART

*6 months later*

"We'll have to postpone the wedding again. It's a bad business but I won't have you walk down the aisle on the arm of a cripple." Jacques was pushing the stem of his glass over the mahogany tabletop. The honey-colored liquid, his third scotch, created miniature waves in the crystal-cut glass. It sputtered and sparkled, sending tiny rays of light into the trail of smoke that rose from the cigarette between his fingers.

Agnès followed the light that reflected from the diamond in his signet ring with her eyes, listening to the words he wasn't saying.

His face was worse than a thundercloud, his brown hair hanging over one dark, ominous eye while he smoked one cigarette after the other. She knew how worried he was about the lack of progress he was making at the revalidation center. His right leg refused to obey him the way he wanted, and this somehow sparked off the old Jacques, moody, morose, blaming others for his own invalidity.

It was hard to be patient with him. She knew she had to. Just a little longer. But it was almost impossible to be around him when he was so helpless while at the same time refusing to be helped. She wasn't worried about the postponement of their wedding. That was the least of her worries. She was worried about *him*, about his fickle state of mind, his dark and brooding moods, his loneliness.

Sighing deeply, she urged herself to give a little more of herself. This phase would pass and then their initial flame would flare up again. Hopefully.

"Are you hungry?" Mentioning food might break the spell but he shook his head.

Emptying his glass, he signaled to the waiter for a refill. "Are you?" his voice was flat, the same tone it had in the first weeks after he'd been hit by the German sniper and she had saved his life by carrying out the most complicated operation of her short career. His sister Elle had called him excruciating but Agnès understood the traumas her patients went through, how it affected their mental health while their bodies healed.

So she answered as chirpily as she could. "I am and I am not." As this sounded rather cryptic, she added, "The years of hunger during the war seemed to have derailed the sensors in my stomach."

He nodded, a half-smile, his mind miles away. "What a sorry couple we are. I'm sorry, Agnès. You deserve better."

"Don't say that. We're in this together."

He greedily drank from the glass the waiter put in front of him, totally immersing him in his life liquid.

The young man in the long white apron cleared his throat, not forgetting his task. "Madame?" One hand behind his back, his other gloved hand holding the tray, he waited politely for her order.

Agnès shook her head. She had hardly touched her first glass of white wine. "I'm fine, thank you."

The waiter made a slight bow before he with- drew to his counter.

Jacques grumbled an angry, "I'm even forgetting my manners. Sorry, Agnès, being corrected by that oaf. It's humiliating."

She refrained from saying anything. What was there to say? They felt lonely apart and lonely together. Marriage would hopefully bring a change to that.

It wasn't just his invalidity, Agnès knew it was also the four long years of war at Château de Dragancourt that had weighed Jacques down. He just wasn't the kind of person who knew how to process all the mutilations and deaths that had happened under his roof. As if anyone knew how to come to terms with the massacre. Anyone. But in Jacques it all boiled and festered inside, unable to attach words to how the war had not just ravaged his earldom but his very soul.

And then there was Elle, whom he missed dearly. Elle had followed Abigail to the States and now lived with her in New York, shunning France and the past. Her past had also been his. It slowly killed all Jacques's joy in life, turning him into a sourpuss. Agnès had no more tools to help him, to turn his misery around. It was slowly but certainly beginning to erode her optimism as well.

*Damn the war!* she often thought. *Damn that world war that has not just taken a whole generation of young able men from us but has maimed millions more, robbing them of a future they could have had, should have had.*

She loved Jacques and he loved her. There was no doubt about it, but was it going to be enough? Taking a sip from the citric wine, she felt gloom settling on her as well. She so needed a little cheerfulness and support herself. Especially tonight, as they were supposed to celebrate their six months as a couple.

"We should set a preliminary date. I think it would perk us both up."

"I'm not sure about that anymore." Jacques emptied another glass, his hands shaking uncontrollably, his next cigarette landing on the table instead of between his lips. "I can't do this to you, Agnès. I'm a wreck. You need something better than a wreck."

"You're not telling me …" Her voice stopped in midair; her throat clamping shut like the shells of an oyster. He couldn't be doing this to her, not after all they had come through together. Through misty eyes she saw him nod as if in slow-motion.

"That's what I've come to conclude here in this miserable establishment off Trocadero." His voice sounded clipped but with more resolution than she'd heard in months. He drained another drink, very drunk now. "I am here to give you your liberty, Agnès Gúnarssón. Let's part in love before this whole thing becomes too ugly and we will never be able to look each other in the face again."

Agnès was too stricken to utter a word. She sat very still, a deep sense of rejection slowly filling up her body. She had kissed this man; she had promised herself to him. And she hadn't done that lightly. And now she was told that he wouldn't marry her after all. Yet, within all that hurt there was a grain of sanity. Liberty? What did it mean? Not having to fight every hour for a man who was sinking, who used her as driftwood. Liberty. Going out with Katell again. Being with her family without the shadow of a depressed Jacques hanging over her every move.

But her lips formed the words, "I can't leave you, Jacques. I'm not sure what will happen to you."

For the first time he straightened up and made eye contact with her, beautiful but bloodshot eyes, somehow clearer than they had been before he sank into one of his drinking sessions. "If you promise you will always love the good in me, I promise you I'll seek help and get my pitiful self out of this self-depreciating mess. I promise."

"You know I love you, Jacques." It was barely more than a whisper.

"Then please remain my North Star, Agnès Gunárssón, my fairy Baroness, my inspiration to be a better man. But be free to love someone worthy of your love. And that, sadly, is not me."

"Are you sure? Or are you just drunk?" She had to ask.

"I'm both."

Something clicked into place. A talk she'd had with her father the night before.

*"Are you sure, my DEAR, THAT he's the MAN for you?"*

Knowing her father would never stand in the way of her happiness, she had protested loudly at this seed of doubt. Now she understood. Loving someone lasted a lifetime but it didn't necessarily mean marriage. Hadn't Papa loved her mother though they had never been together?

Love.

Such a big word.

Becoming aware of Jacques' presence next to her again, her brain flipped through all the pictures with him since she'd been fifteen. This world-wise teenager, so handsome, so fickle, so out of reach. He had put his kingdom at her feet, but it was before he had lost it. What had he done to her? Stirring all these contradictory emotions in her, always making her feel at edge. Just like with Elle, despite the fact that his maleness had confused her even more.

Love or confusion?

She was no longer sure. "So what do we do now?" "I'm going to a rehab clinic in Switzerland. Then

I may travel again and write another book."

"Is that really what you want, Jacques? And what about me?"

Jacques let out a dry, mirthless laugh. "I'm not a wise man by any means, my dear Agnès, but this I know. You'll find your happiness one day. You're made for happiness. I'll sail by as best as I can. But my fate is so different from yours. Happiness may not be part of the equation."

There it was again. The melancholic outlook that always nibbled at her heart when she was with him. With sudden clarity, she knew he was right. Their love wasn't meant to result in marriage. How had she never seen that?

"So when will you leave?"

"First thing in the morning."

"Will you write?"

"Of course, every word I'll ever write will be for you, my love." Jacques gestured to the waiter to get the bill.

Soon they stood facing each other, the looming Eiffel tower casting a long-drawn shadow over the evening street. It was almost midnight. Paris had burst into spring with blossoms and buoyancy. Post-war Paris had revived.

"Let me embrace you one more time." Jacques shivered in his summer coat, looking gaunt and ill.

Agnès let his arms surround her, feeling his warmth, his tender love for her. They were both crying, their souls melting in what they had lost. "I'll always love you but thank you for setting me free."

Those were her last words. Until they would meet again.

∼

*A YEAR LATER*

The bells of Notre Dame clanged with loud bangs through the crystalline Spring air, inviting the faithful inside for Mass. Agnès walked with swift steps towards Madame Ringard's flower stall on the left bank of the Seine. Today was her stepsister's Freya's fifteen's birthday and the Melancourt family was preparing for a party.

Freya's birthday also meant the last week before the

baron and his family set off for their two-month trip to Sweden. Without Agnès these days. She couldn't take that long off from her work at the American Hospital. And though she missed visiting the country of her birth, she also liked having the house to herself. She was twenty-five now, still young but also mature enough to look after herself.

Today she had taken the day off, though, to help Mme Proulx prepare the festivities and spend the precious last full day with her reconstituted family. A soft breeze played with her blond hair, while her light eyes scanned the bustling crowds around her, meanwhile filling her lungs with all the Paris morning had to offer her. The tangy scent of Seine water, gasoline from passing cars and omnibuses, wafts of freshly baked croissants and black coffee. How she loved Paris. It was the center of her universe.

Bending her head over the lilies and roses at Madame Ringard's stall, she inhaled their perfume while her eyes feasted on the colors and shapes.

"I think pink roses, carnations and baby's breath," she murmured as she heard a deep voice behind her say, "Red roses!" Turning to see who was addressing her, her face broke into a surprised smile. "Professor Bell! I had no idea you were back in Paris. Thought you had returned to the States for good."

"Doctor Agnès!" The tall thirtyish American let his intense gray eyes rest on her, a trace of amusement and warmth in them. "How good to see you again. Yes, I returned. Paris can easily do without me, but I can't do without Paris. Took me a year to figure that out."

It felt so natural hearing him talk in that Midwest

accent of his, so different from the Oxford English of her former tutor. She'd missed working and conversing with her former professor. There was always so much to learn from him.

"So will you be lecturing at the Sorbonne again?"

"Part-time! But hey, do you have a moment? I'd love to chat over coffee with you. Catch up on everything."

"Sure, let me just pay for these flowers." She looked down on the huge bouquet in her arms.

Without giving her a chance to protest, he grabbed the entire bucket of Madame Ringard's red roses with one hand and the flowers in her arms with the other. "Deliver this to the Baron's house, while I take *Madame Docteur* for coffee."

He handed the florist a wad of Franc notes while winking at Agnès. "It's all on me. To express how glad I am to bump into you of all Parisians on my return. I couldn't have asked for a more suitable companion. And I have news!"

He guided her to a café-bar on the Quai de Montebello, where they sat down at a table on the outdoor terrace. Agnès's mind raced. She would have thirty minutes at the most, having promised Mrs. Proulx to help her with decorating Freya's birthday cake. And their guests would be arriving for lunch.

It was strange suddenly sitting here in the sunshine on an ordinary Wednesday morning with her former professor. He had taught her and Katell all the surgery they performed during the war, some- times even with his written instructions at hand. Her skillful, patient teacher. That quaint but friendly American who'd told them female specialists were the future of the medical profession.

How wrong he'd been. After the war most trained women had returned to their stoves, leaving specialist jobs to their male counterparts, and the government seemed to encourage this. At least *she* hadn't failed Professor Bell's hope for the future, and neither had Katell. They still worked side by side in the American Hospital.

Alan Bell had returned to Chicago immediately after Armistice Day and she had lost track of him since. They had only known each other during the siege. Now it was peace. She had matured, known hardship and heartbreak. She wasn't the girl anymore whose hand he held steady to make her first stitches on the first wounded soldier on her operation table. Thousands of stitches had followed since. Some successful, some not so.

Aware they had both remained silent until it became awkward, she opened her mouth.

He did so at the same time. "How have you been?"

It sounded like any physician's neutral question but there was an urgency behind it. A need for them to fill the blanks, to gauge the mental stability of a fellow doctor after a prolonged crisis.

Agnès felt herself breathe freely after a very long time. Here was someone who knew what she'd really endured, what she had stood for and what price she had paid for it. She gazed into his eyes and what she saw warmed her soul. Admiration and pride, but there was something else; he'd come back to tell her something. Had he not said so?

"What is it?" Her voice faltered, suddenly feeling quite emotional.

"It's you two, Docteur Agnès Gunarsson de Melancourt, and Docteur Katell Brest. Do you remember a soldier by the name of Corporal Peter Swift?"

She was puzzled. "Of course, I remember him. He was our very last patient at Dragancourt. A Texan. What about him?"

"Well, the good man didn't rest until President Woodrow decided to decorate you and Katell for your war efforts. They contacted me to ask if you still worked at the American Hospital. When the request came, I knew I had to come back here. I knew I belonged in Paris, my second home. With you, with the staff."

"So you're really back?" Agnes's eyes lit up, temporarily forgetting any high American decorations. She'd already been given the Croix de Guerre and that was quite enough for her. Alan back with the team was *excellent* news.

"I am. But only under one condition."

"Being?"

"That you run the place with me. It's time we had a young female on the board among all the male doctors. I'd actually hoped to tell you under more ceremonial circumstances, you know, when you walked into the hospital tomorrow morning, but then ..." He stopped for a moment before continuing, "... the spirit of the Notre Dame in her infinite wisdom made sure we met on this God-given day. I know you don't like to be surprised."

Agnès was dumbfounded, while pride welled up in her breast at the same time. Being promoted to the board, at twenty-five, it was simply unconceivable. How proud her father would be. Then her shoulders slumped as she slowly shook her head.

"What is it, Agnès?" Alan grabbed her hand, long slender surgeon fingers wrapping around hers. "Ah, I think I know what it is, but don't worry. There is place for two females on the board." He gave her fingers a small squeeze.

Her face became instant sunshine. She had to prevent herself from embracing him in her enthusiasm. "You mean...?"

"Yes, Docteur Brest will be invited as well. It was actually a prerequisite by Professor Briard who is retiring this month. He's been watching the two of you. Closely and meticulously. You're both more than ready, he assured me."

Agnès glanced at her Elgin pocket watch. She really needed to go. Her family was waiting.

Alan threw another wad of franc bank notes on the table before following her into the street. "Have dinner with me tomorrow night. To celebrate."

His face held an almost boyish yearning, a side of him she'd not seen before. It made her heart stir as if it was waking up from a long winter sleep.

*Silly goose, he's pROBABLY MARRIED. He's just trying to be nice.*

Agnès nodded, just a slight jerk of her head, but his lean, clean-shaven face lit up at her consent. Gray eyes sparkled as his smile broadened. "But first the official instalment tomorrow morning."

She nodded again. "I'm so glad my family is still in Paris. My father is sure to make a great fuss out of this."

"And so he should! And you and I have a deal?"

"We have!"

Agnès floated home through the Paris morning as if she had wings. All was well again. She was at peace. Finally at peace.

~

DID YOU ENJOY *DOCTOR AGNÈS*? Do you agree with her love choice?

Read the full story of Agnès and Alan in In Picardy's Fields. It follows a slightly different path but "In Picardy's Fields" is their real story!

So turn the page...

# FIRST CHAPTER "IN PICARDY'S FIELDS"

## Chapter 1 Two Men

**Paris, March 1918**

THE LATE AFTERNOON sun set ablaze the upper windows of the operation room in the Lycée Pasteur, creating a golden aureole over the electric lamps that illuminated the wounded soldier on the table and the medical staff around him.

There was a concentrated silence in the room, interrupted only by the faint hissing of the Heidbrink anesthetizer gas machine and the short commands Professor Alan Bell issued from behind his surgical mask: *Harmonic scalpel ... retractor... lancet*, which were promptly handed to him by the American nurse at his side.

From the other side of the table, the young assistant doctor Agnès de Saint-Aubin followed the surgeon's swift and practiced hands as he removed the bullet from the patient's neck. There was an intense, steady focus in her blue eyes.

"*Voilà!* Another 5mm bullet from those bloody G98s." For a moment, Dr. Bell studied the round ball between his tweezers before depositing it in a metal tray that the nurse held ready. It clattered, metal hitting metal.

"More oxygen... antiseptics!" The surgeon had already moved to the next stage.

Agnès knew how complicated and dangerous this gunshot wound was. It had hit the young French soldier at high velocity, and the trajectory of the bullet had damaged his nervous system. He was bleeding profusely and was greatly in need of a blood transfusion, which another nurse was hastily preparing. With the strong medicinal odor of the chlorine prickling her nostrils, Agnès let her gaze rest for a moment on the young man's still profile, the roman nose, the dark, almost girlish eyelashes over his closed lids, black locks of matted hair emerging from under his operation cap. He still retained a vague glow of health under his ashen color. How old was he? Seventeen, eighteen? What had he dreamt of achieving in this war? And what would become of him now?

"Stitch him up, Doctor de Saint-Aubin, and when you're done, come and see me in the canteen."

Agnès startled. Her eyes met those of her American professor, and she thought she saw a softening in the steel-gray gaze.

"Of course, Professor Bell, right away." Her words were more straightforward than her voice, but she hastened around the table to take up his position next to the stout nurse. The head surgeon had already removed the white cap from his brown curls and was now snapping off his surgical gloves. With his gaze still on Agnès, he gave his last orders to the nurse.

"Nurse Simpson, assist the new doctor. Make sure you check her multilayer sutures. Nurse Belliard, blood transfusion – now!"

"Yes, Professor Bell," both nurses answered, while Agnès took a deep breath and ceased following the movements of her professor to give all her attention to the young patient on the table. His life; not hers.

She heard him disappear through the swinging doors that flapped for a couple of times before falling still. Agnès took another deep breath, steadying her hands before she said in a subdued voice, "Needle..."

The American nurse, ready to exert a maternal preponderance over this inexperienced doctor, instantly handed her the bent needle and thread. In an upbeat voice, she added, "You'll do all right, Doctor."

This kind nudge gave Agnès the confidence she needed, and she completed the complicated sutures under the older woman's scrutiny, knowing she was doing the best job at stitching she had done so far.

While she was washing her hands at the enamel sink in the kitchen unit next to the operation room, she heard the screeching wheels of the hospital bed as the patient was wheeled to the recovery room. She hoped he would live and convalesce completely but knew his chances were slim. So many had already died under her hands. She reminded herself of the next step in the process; no more thinking of the patient at this point.

She should be proud. She had done well, blocking her emotions during the operation and especially during her own suturing. She was making progress. Professor Bell's lessons were finally sinking in; she was developing a neutral attitude to suffering and complications. Agnès smiled at herself. She could hear him say it in that American tongue of his, pronouncing his r's and long, drawling vowels, an English so exotically different from that of her Oxford English tutor.

"Doctor de Saint-Aubin, there is no difference between a male and a female surgeon. Emotions simply stay out of the operation room. Always."

Drying her hands on the red-checked tea towel, she wondered what his reason was for summoning her to the canteen. They had never met outside the lecture room or the operation theater, so Agnès felt uneasy. She was mastering the work; simply doing the job, identical to cutting and stitching dummies during the lectures. Truth was that her stomach still felt queasy after every operation – no matter that Professor Bell had told her she was cut from a special cloth; that female surgeons were going to be the stars of the twentieth century. He had taken it upon himself to personally supervise her surgical progress after she obtained her *Diplôme de l'Etat de docteur en medicine* from l'Université de Sorbonne in the spring of 1914; first at the American Hospital in Paris and now as part of his operation team at the Lycée Pasteur. Nothing pointed to him being dissatisfied with her. So, what now?

She suppressed a sudden thrill that he might ask her out. There had never been anything but a professional contact between them, and he was – of course –

almost a decade older than she was, somewhere in his early thirties.

"Silly goose, he's probably married. Although he doesn't wear a wedding band. But who does in the operation room?" As she smoothed her springy blonde hair on top of her head and gave her full lips a dash of coral lipstick, she noticed how pale and tired she looked, with dark rings under her eyes, her face pale from the rationing and working long hours. How would he ever notice her if she looked so mousy? To add some color to her cheeks, she gave them both a soft pinch, and then gazed at her own eyes. They were an intense soft blue; *robin's egg blue,* Papa called them. If only she looked a little darker, more French – which was a ridiculous wish as everyone always complimented her on her pale, elflike look. But the Americans loved the dark-haired French girls. She saw it all around her.

Smoothing the dark-green pleats of her day dress, Agnès hastened through the long corridors of the Lycée Pasteur, originally built as a school for Neuilly-sur-Seine but now temporarily turned into an exten- sion of the American War Hospital because the ongoing war demanded more emergency beds every day. Temporarily? It had been going on for close to four years now, and it only seemed to get worse. Outside in the Lycée's courtyard, the blue vans of the American Ambulance Field Service came and went in parade, with never a lull in the arrival of wounded men from the front. But for today, her day at the operation table was over.

Before entering the canteen, Agnès paused for a moment. Doctor Bell had always been honest with her, so there was no reason to think she had muddled things up. Chin up, she told herself.

The hospital canteen was the only place in the 1600-bed hospital that offered a relatively warm space to relax and recuperate. It was a large, whitewashed room with a high, beamed ceiling and a row of tall alcove windows along the Boulevard d'Inkermann letting in plenty of light during the day. Around the clock, the canteen was a beehive of comings and goings, filled to the ridge with the smoke of hundreds of pipes and cigarettes, the chatter of voices, the clinking of cutlery and the scraping of wooden chairs over the sanded floorboards. On both sides of the long tables, the electric bulbs above them looming as over- sized pearls, a variety of nationalities sat side by side. Medical staff, ambulance drivers, recovering soldiers, they all shared just one goal: to win the war against Imperial Germany.

Agnès saw Alan Bell standing near the soup table, engrossed in animated conversation with one of the pretty American Red Cross nurses. His hand touched her arm lightly at times, and he nodded at her while the brunette gazed up at him, recounting what must have been a funny story as they both laughed heartily. Hesitantly, Agnès approached, not sure whether she should interrupt their conversation, but Alan spotted her and gestured to her to come closer.

"Doctor de Saint-Aubin, come and meet Elsie Gamble. She's from Chicago, like me! We grew up on the same street. Now, isn't that a coincidence?"

Agnès noted how he called the nurse by her first

name while addressing her formally, but when she shook the girl's soft white hand, Elsie smiled warmly.

"So nice to meet you, Doctor de Saint-Aubin. I won't tell you all the good things Al's just told me about you." *Wink, wink.* "I'm ever so impressed to meet a female surgeon in the flesh. But right now, I should get my lazy behind out of the way, as my shift's starting in ten minutes."

With an amicable slap to Alan's arm, she moved away. Her round hips swayed slightly under her white nurse's coat, a fact that did not go unnoticed by the soldiers in the room, whose weary faces brightened whenever they caught a glimpse of female beauty. Just like the Americans and Brits liked the French girls, the Frenchmen were infatuated with American nurses, who were known to be ever so carefree and spontaneous.

"Sit over there." Alan pointed to a table in the corner that was slightly less crowded. "I'll get us something. Would you like some soup, or toast with scrambled eggs?"

"Just a café au lait and a biscuit, please."

Alan looked at her with one dark eyebrow raised. "Still not steady on the nerves? I won't insist, but after eight hours at the operation table, you do need to eat a little more than a cookie, Doctor de Saint-Aubin."

"I will, in a minute. But first, coffee. And please, call me Agnès."

She watched him order himself a full plate of beef bourguignon and a large mug of tea. He moved with such ease, such composure, speaking French to the fat cook as if he had lived in her country all his life. It had become second nature to her – minutely studying his expressions and movements – but so far it had only been a logical process of learning from him in the operating theater. As this was the first time seeing him interact with others outside the medical sphere, it was a novelty to her but she studied it all just the same.

He came towards her, balancing his food and her coffee on the metal tray, and she noticed the smile had disappeared from his hand- some face.

"I'm ravenous," he announced. "I do have something important to tell you, but could it wait a couple of minutes until I've wolfed this down?"

"Of course." Agnès stirred her coffee, steadying her queasy stomach against the strong smell of beef that wafted her way. She intentionally diverted her attention to other people at their table to stop herself from scrutinizing him. When he had put down his fork and wiped his mouth on the linen napkin, her eyes met his again. She was aware she must have looked puzzled, but she could not read his intentions. He seemed to be struggling with something, and for a moment, her heart thumped in her throat.

"I'll call you Agnès if you agree to call me Alan." His voice had lost the professorial tone, but it was flat and devoid of emotion.

She nodded, waiting.

He took a sip of his tea as if weighing his words. "I wanted to tell you that I'm leaving Lycée Pasteur to move to a base hospital at the front."

She still did not reply, but looked down at her coffee cup to hide her disappointment.

"There are two reasons for this, Agnès. The first is

that I want to make a real difference in this war – to give it my all, saving lives where it matters most. And secondly, I want to study the major leaps in medical progress where they really happen. And that's at the front. The war is proving to be a great teacher to us doctors."

With some difficulty, Agnès raised her head again. "Why are you telling me this?"

He gave a short, dry laugh. "I didn't just want to disappear. It didn't seem right. You've been my student for four years, and I've been your practical supervisor for the past year. So, the time is right. You're ready to take over from me. You're a good surgeon, Agnès."

"I want..." she started, but then stopped, diverting her gaze again. An awkward silence crept up between them. "I'd like some scrambled eggs on toast now."

"Good choice." He jumped up, giving her space to collect her thoughts. Although she had seen dozens of Allied surgeons departing to the field hospitals closer to the front, it had not occurred to her that Alan might go as well. After all, he oversaw the entire operating team in Paris. But everything was changing. Maybe he was right. Maybe she wanted to go too, and be where she could make a real difference, help the heavy casualties, save lives on the spot.

Agnès's brain worked hard. It was not the first time she had thought about going closer to the battlefields. When the war started, her father and she had made plans to turn their château near Roye into a field hospital, but the Germans had prevented that by seizing the castle during the First Battle of Picardy in September

1914, and since then, its medieval fate hung unknowingly in the air.

Alan returned with her meal and suggested she take her turn eating while he smoked a cigarette.

Having made her decision to ask him to take her with him, Agnès picked up her knife and fork. "You're not in a hurry?"

He waved his hand, dispersing the smoke. "No, not at all. Got all evening. I planned to take a walk along the Seine. Could do with some relative peace before the real madness starts. Care to come along?"

Agnès smiled. "I'd love to!" She had eaten a few bites and pushed her plate aside. Resting her elbows on the tablecloth, she asked in her quiet voice, "Can I come with you to the front?"

For a moment he seemed baffled, then curtly said "No!" while extinguishing his cigarette in the overfull ashtray with a firm jab.

But Agnès was not that easily pushed aside. "Why not, Alan?" Saying his Christian name was an unusual experience, but it felt invigorating.

He jumped to his feet. "Let's take that walk, and I'll explain why."

From the Lycée Pasteur, they walked along the rue Peronnet in the direction of the Seine. The March sun had already sunk behind the tall buildings, and leaden clouds gathered in the sky signaled rain in the evening. They did not speak, and Agnès was painfully aware of Alan's proximity, the tall man by her side who did his best to curb his big strides so she could keep up with him. He was at least two heads taller than she and walked with that American swagger Agnès so admired in him and his countrymen, as if they still needed to secure their supremacy over the Wild West.

Not knowing what to say but dying to ask questions, she decided to remain quiet as well, telling herself to just enjoy the opportunity of being with him. When they reached the boulevard that ran along the Seine with busy traffic going both ways – taxis, private automobiles, army vehicles, ambulances – Alan turned to her.

"Which way?"

"I live two miles to the left, near the Pont de Puteaux. Would you like to go in that direction for a bit?"

"You live near the Bois de Boulogne?" He sounded surprised, then added with an endearing chuckle, "ah, that's right, you're a Baroness. Had quite forgotten that. Gosh, you Europeans! Truly never met so much old blood before in my life. Every other person I speak to is a Viscount or an Earl of something."

Agnès bit her tongue but decided not to tell him she was not a Baroness by birth but had been adopted. "Would you like to walk along the waterside?" she suggested.

"Sure."

They descended the stone steps and went along the broad pave- ment, with boats and smaller barges gliding past in the diffuse after noon light. The green spur of the Île de la Jatte was to their right. Agnès breathed in deeply. She liked taking this route home, close to the river, after a long day in the operation room. There was a fresh breeze in every season here, and the pungent scent of the water, cool as a mountain stream, always livened her senses. The dark water rippled in miniature waves, sloshing against the quay when larger boats passed. Green patches of vegetation drifted by, and silver-finned fish skittered under the surface.

They still walked in silence, each wrapped in their own thoughts. Agnès took regular, precise steps, her arms by her sides, her medical bag clutched in her right hand, while Alan, who walked hatless with his brown locks pushed away from his forehead, had his hands folded at his back.

Just when Agnès wondered if she should break the silence because it was becoming awkward, he said evenly, "Listen, Agnès, I had it all worked out. You've trained under me long enough to lead the team at the Lycée. That was my reason for waiting to go up north – to make sure you'd be ready."

She was baffled by his words, but her heart swelled with pride at this promotion. "Thank you. I honestly didn't know you had so much confidence in me."

"I trained you, remember?" Again, that chuckle she had never heard in the operation room. It made him sound younger, more boyish.

"True." She gave him a shy smile, her eyes catching the last of the evening light.

"So, it would be rather inconvenient if you also decided to leave for the front."

"Doctor Davies could take charge."

Alan seemed to ponder this for a moment. "He might."

"It's not a whim, Alan. I've been considering this ever since the war started." And she told him of the sad circumstances of Château de Saint-Aubin.

He listened attentively but shook his head. "I'm not your father, just your mentor and supervisor, but if I *were* your father, I would simply forbid it." The stern professorial tone was back.

Agnès sighed. "I'm sure my father will be in total agreement with you. But what about the rumors that the Germans are considering a new offensive on the Western Front, now that Russia is no longer in the war? They could take Paris overnight, and I wouldn't be safe here either then."

"Then you could flee south, like everyone else will."

"As long as this wicked war goes on, nobody is safe anywhere," Agnès remarked bitterly.

"But there's a difference between seeking danger and staying relatively safe."

"The same goes for you."

Agnès wondered how it was possible she was talking in this manner to her professor, but somehow their walking together in civilian clothes with the bustle of her own city all around them made her ignore the distance they had always carefully observed. And she could not bear the thought of never working with him again. She was not done learning from him; she wanted more, more than this. So she decided to try one more thing.

"We're almost there. Would you care to come and meet my father, to see how he thinks about this ludicrous plan of mine?" She made it sound as light-hearted as she could.

Alan glanced at his pocket watch and then looked

at the sky where the clouds were thickening. "I think I ought to be..."

"Please, Alan."

He glanced at her begging face then shrugged his shoulders in a comical way. "Oh, all right, then. I suppose I owe you something after all this time working together. If you want to fight two men, be my guest. Show us what you're worth." He grinned at her, and for a moment she felt incredibly close to him.

They left the pathway along the Seine at the Pont de Puteaux, and after crossing the Boulevard de la Seine, Agnès directed them to a stately mansion on the waterfront. The dark-green front door read in decorative golden lettering *Baron Maximilien de Saint-Aubin et famille.*

As soon as she opened the door with her latchkey, the housekeeper Madame Petit appeared from the front parlor looking questioningly at Agnès. "You're all right, Miss Agnès? You're very late!"

"Sure, Petipat, everything's fine. This is Professor Bell. Is Papa home?"

The ample-bosomed housekeeper nodded, straightening her massive black dress, and looked, slightly bewildered, from the young girl to the tall American who was standing rather stiffly on the doormat.

"Yes, yes, of course. Do come in, Professor Bell. Welcome." Busying herself with making room for them in the parlor, puffing up cushions and rearranging chairs, she addressed the young Baroness but secretly eyed Alan, giving Agnès inward glee at the effort the elderly woman was making at understanding what was going on.

"The Baron is in his music room, as usual," the housekeeper went on. "He was waiting for you, as he'll be going out tonight. Will you be going out as well, Miss Agnès?"

"No, Petipat, it's been a long day. Afternoon shift tomorrow, but still early bed for me." She glanced up at Alan, wondering what would happen tomorrow. He had not told her if he was leaving straight away.

"Now, I'll go and fetch your father, my girl." Moving as fast as her voluminous body allowed her, the housekeeper proposed before she disappeared in the hallway, "Do make yourselves at home, dears, and tell me what I can get you."

"Would you care for a sherry, Alan? Or maybe something stronger? My father wisely stocked his cellars before the war. We may run out of potatoes, but we've still got plenty of liquor." She giggled.

"A sherry will be fine, Ma'am," Alan said politely, but as soon as the housekeeper had left, he lifted a quizzical eyebrow. "Petipat?"

"Oh, do sit down." Agnès laughed. "It's just my special name for her. She's been like a mother to me."

"Ah, I see. So, your own mother...?" Agnès nodded and hoped Alan would not probe any further in this sensitive matter, but after a while the silence hung heavily in the room, so she added timidly, "My mother died shortly after giving birth to me. I was raised by my father and Madame Petit, who has been with our family since the beginning of time."

"So sorry to hear that." Alan's brow softened with empathy. "If it's any comfort to you, I also lost my mother, though I have some vague memories of her as I was four at the time. My father remarried soon after, but I've never liked my stepmother, whom I was supposed to call Mother as well, and...well ...it's also influenced the relationship with my father." He stared wistfully at the blunt knives on the wall.

Agnès' kind heart went out to him immediately. "My time to be sorry. At least I've had a doting dad, and of course Petipat who's picked me up more times than I can remember."

The air lifted, and she followed Alan's eyes as they took in the room. She wondered what he would make of it and how different it certainly must be from his American house back home, with the parents to whom he did not feel close.

As all the rooms in the De Saint-Aubin household, this one displayed a mishmash of styles, ranging from conservative classic to quirky exotic, very much like the owner himself. The downstairs parlor mostly held objects from the Baron's many trips to the African continent, so it was generally referred to as 'The African room'; other rooms being labeled 'The West Indies Room' and 'The Aboriginal Room.'

The majority of the furniture consisted of high-backed Louis Quinze chairs and canopies in cream chintz, but the coffee table was a wooden elephant carrying a glass plate on its back, and there were a number of rackety stools, carved antelopes, and naked ebony statues, reminiscent of his expeditions into dark Africa. The floor was carpeted with Persian rugs, but here and there the skin of a lion or a tiger had been thrown on top of them, trophies from his safari trips. Oval ancestor portraits were juxtaposed with spears, knives, and other primitive weaponry. It was chaotic, personal, liberal. Agnès feared it gave her guest quite a glimpse into her unusual background.

In a room upstairs, a violin abruptly stopped playing, and a little later, voices could be heard coming closer. Alan rose to his feet, thereby hitting his head against one of the low-hanging candelabras.

"You're okay?"

He nodded, rubbing the crown of his head. "Damn height. Never seem to get used to it." At that moment, the Baron entered, with

Madame Petit on his heels, followed by a maid carrying a tray with glasses and a carafe filled with amber-colored sherry.

Her father, although of modest height, at least compared to Alan, managed – as always – to immediately fill the room with his presence. It was not that Baron Maximilien de Saint-Aubin was a remarkably handsome man, nor very imposing, but there was a quality in his posture, a mixture of what Alan had called 'old blood' and a personal artistic freedom, that made certain no one overlooked him. It was in the way he moved, elastic like a cat yet aristocratic in his uprightness, the elegant movements of his arms derived from a life-long practice as a musician, and the ease with which he carried himself, confident but never completely in tune with protocol and decorum. He had the creaseless olive-colored skin from his Spanish mother and the silver-streaked hair and honey-brown eyes of his late father, the 6th Baron de Saint-Aubin.

His clothing was always of good quality and often had a colorful, eccentric twist. Today he was wearing embroidered Persian *babouches*, simple charcoal flannel trousers with a clear fold in them, and a dark- blue pullover under which the collar of his white chemise, with the invariably colorful silk cravat tucked in.

A broad smile spread over his mustached face as he approached them, and it was typical of the Baron that he first went over to his daughter to plant a kiss on her fair forehead and compliment her on her loveliness before turning on his heels and greeting their guest. Agnès knew why he did this – to make clear that any man who might be interested in her would have to deal with the father first, but it embarrassed her as it was rude to Alan, who after all was her professor. And since she was twenty-three, there was really no reason for him to treat her as a little girl.

"Ahh, Professor Bell! Agnès has told me so much about you. Glad to finally make your acquaintance." He shook Alan's hand cordially and then seated himself in one of the Louis Quinze armchairs, putting one knee over the other and rearranging the flannel crease so it went straight over his knee.

Alan sat back down on the coach. Agnès noticed an uncertainty in him she had not seen before, and she inwardly cursed her father. He made a habit of making other people feel smaller than needed. While the maid handed round glasses, she decided she would come to the point straightaway, so Alan did not need to stay in her house any longer than he probably wanted.

"Papa, Alan... uh... Professor Bell is here for a reason, as you might have guessed." Her father took a contemplative sip from his glass and set it down on the side table before looking up at her.

"Alan?" he asked in mock surprise, "Oh... I see. Yes, of course. You have been working together for so long it is probably appropriate by now." And turning to Alan, he added, "You're American, are you?"

"Yes, sir, originally from Chicago, but I moved to Paris in 1910 after graduating from Harvard Medical School *summa cum laude.*"

*Ha,* Agnès thought, *you know how to deal with my father. You're one up on him.* But she remembered Alan had told her that he wanted to see her fight two men, so before her father could further digress on a topic of Americans versus Europeans, she interrupted.

"Papa, this is not a polite visit. It has a specific purpose. I want to ask your permission for something."

"Fire away, my darling!"

"Alan has decided to leave the American Hospital in Paris to work closer to the front. I want to go too."

The Baron took another sip from his glass, biding his time, and Agnès was curious to see which angle he would take. He cleared his throat and fixing his brown gaze on Alan, calmly remarked, "Noble decision. I'm all for it. Where exactly are you going?"

"I was thinking of the American base hospital no 5. in the Pas de Calais, but I have been invited to several others."

The Baron nodded. "You must have been. With your expertise, they'll be lining up for you. Sad business, this war. Only engineers and doctors seem to benefit from it, making one invention after the other. Still, all these novel ideas will come in useful in peacetime, no doubt." He sighed, and Agnès waited.

"Listen, Professor Bell. I'm not at all involved in

warfare. I do my humble bit at the Ministry of Food Supplies and in supporting Clemenceau, that sort of thing, but that's about as far as my knowledge goes. However, my good friend Count Horace de Dragoncourt – Agnès here knows him too – is the French ambassador in London, and he also owns a château near Amiens that has been turned into a Red Cross hospital. His eldest children, slightly older than my girl, are in charge, although they aren't doctors. Just yesterday I received a letter from Horace complaining they are desperately short of surgeons, which isn't surprising, I suppose."

The Baron gave a scornful laugh and took another sip before he continued. "Well... you see... if you're not damned set on going to be with your fellow countrymen at the Pas de Calais, you could consider taking a look at Dragoncourt instead. It would give you the extra bonus of visiting one of the greatest French renaissance chateaus, though, by Deuce, what's left of its splendor is anybody's guess." The Baron's face darkened, and Agnès knew he was thinking of their own castle in Picardy.

Alan asked, "How many beds do they have?"

"My dear chap, I have no idea, but I can find out for you."

This was Agnès's chance to interrupt. "If Alan decides to go to Dragoncourt, would you let me go as well?"

The Baron shifted his legs, placing the other knee on top, and now

started studying the crease. When he looked up again, his voice was composed and friendly but held an undertone of alarm. "You're safer here and ... and you know why."

"No, Papa, I am not!" Her voice sounded shrill. "I'm not afraid, and I have nothing to hide!"

The Baron glanced at Alan, who was observing both father and daughter, and he added hastily, "I don't see a way around it, my sweet girl."

Agnès rose, her lips pressed together, lacing her delicate, thin fingers in front of her stomach until her knuckles showed white.

"I'll let Alan out. But you know, Papa, that we intended to turn Château de Saint-Aubin into a front-line hospital before it was seized by the Germans, so I don't understand your objection now." In all honesty, she had to admit she did understand, but what was safe these days? Nothing.

Both men rose as well, Alan carefully avoiding the candelabra. The Baron shook his head wearily. "I would have joined you to at De Saint- Aubin, Agnès darling, but there's no way I could accompany you to Dragoncourt. That's the difference."

Agnès looked hopefully to Alan. Would he come to her rescue? But she saw he would not. She had lost the battle, and with it she had also lost him.

"You'll be okay, Agnès," Alan said consolingly, as they stood on the steps outside her front door. Agnès wrapped her arms around herself, chilled and defeated. Alan looked so distinguished in the city's evening lights, yet so unattainable. She felt like running up to her room to sob on her bed, but she restrained herself.

"Will I see you before you leave?"

"Of course. I won't be leaving until the end of the

week. Now cheer up, Doctor de Saint-Aubin, you've got your whole future ahead of you."

"Do I?"

Then he did something he had not done before. He grasped her hand and shook it. With the feel of his capable surgeon hand in hers, so warm and strong, she could not but smile, and he smiled back.

Returning to the sitting room, she found her father hiding behind his newspaper, *Le Petit Parisien*. "Alan will be wondering if we're covering something up," she said bitterly.

"No, he won't. He understands I'm protecting you. And if you ask me, he's doing exactly the same."

"You are... you are always so righteous, Papa, but this is wrong! I want to be where I'm needed most."

"You *are* where you're needed most, *mon enfant*!"

Download In Picardy's Fields here. Also in Kindle Unlimited.

# ABOUT THE AUTHOR

**Author's Bio**

Hannah Byron's crib stood near the Seine in Paris, but she was raised in the south of Holland by Anglo-Dutch parents. In her bestselling WW2 historical fiction series, *The Resistance Girl Series*, Hannah's heroines also traipse from one European country to the next, very much like their creator.

Now a retired university lecturer and translator, the European traveler and avid researcher still regularly crosses borders to learn about new vistas.

What started as curiosity about her family's connection to D-Day, evolved into an out-of-controlish study into WW2 history. To blame, or thank, must be Uncle Tom Naylor. If he'd not landed on the beaches of Normandy and helped liberate Holland, her British mother would never have met her Dutch Dad after the war.

Strong women are at the core of Byron's clean and wholesome romance novels. Every book is a tribute to the generation that started the women's lib movement, got dirty in overalls, flew planes, and did intelligence work. Today's girl bosses can but stand on the shoulders of these amazons.

Side-by-side with their male counterparts, Byron's heroines fight for freedom, equality and... love.

Under the pen name Hannah Ivory she writes Historical Mysteries. *The Mrs Imogene Lynch Series* stars the kind but opinionated Victorian widow of Constable Thaddeus Lynch.

## ALSO BY HANNAH BYRON
### HISTORICAL FICTION

**The Resistance Girl Series**

In Picardy's Fields

The Diamond Courier

The Parisian Spy

The Norwegian Assassin

The Highland Raven

The Crystal Butterfly

The London Spymaker (preorder)

Box Set The Resistance Girl Series 1-4

**Spin-off novellas: The Agnès Duet**

Miss Agnès

Doctor Agnès

### HANNAH IVORY
### VICTORIAN MYSTERIES

**The Mrs Imogene Lynch Series**

The Unsolved Case of The Secret Christmas Baby

The Peculiar Vanishing Act of Mr Ralph Herriot (7 Sept. 23)

The Perilous Pursuit for Mr Banerjee's Gemstone (coming soon)

Printed in Great Britain
by Amazon